# TOTALLY MIDDLE SCHOOL

# TOTALLY MIDDLE SCHOOL

## TALES OF FRIENDS, FAMILY, AND FITTING IN

EDITED BY BETSY GROBAN

DELACORTE PRESS

Compilation and introduction copyright © 2018 by Betsy Groban
"Letters" copyright © 2018 by Lois Lowry
"What Planet Are You From?" copyright © 2018 by Gregory Maguire
"When She Whined in Her Sleep" copyright © 2018 by Gary D. Schmidt
"Looking for Home" copyright © 2018 by Karen Cushman
"How to Make S'mores" copyright © 2018 by Hena Khan
"The Skater" copyright © 2018 by Mary Downing Hahn
"Imaginary Mambo" copyright © 2018 by Margarita Engle
"Ode to the Band Room" copyright © 2018 by Joyce Sidman
"TBH I Need HELP!! 🙈" copyright © 2018 by Katherine Paterson and Jordan Paterson
"Dog People" copyright © 2018 by Linda Sue Park and Anna Dobbin
"Middle School" copyright © 2018 by David Wiesner
Jacket art copyright © 2018 by Neil Swaab

All rights reserved. Published in the United States by Delacorte Press, an imprint of Random House Children's Books, a division of Penguin Random House LLC, New York.

Delacorte Press is a registered trademark and the colophon is a trademark of Penguin Random House LLC.

Visit us on the Web! rhcbooks.com

Educators and librarians, for a variety of teaching tools, visit us at RHTeachersLibrarians.com

Library of Congress Cataloging-in-Publication Data is available upon request.
ISBN 978-1-5247-7220-8 (trade)
ISBN 978-1-5247-7221-5 (lib. bdg.)
ISBN 978-1-5247-7222-2 (ebook)

The text of this book is set in xx-point font.
Interior design by Trish Parcell

Printed in the United States of America
10 9 8 7 6 5 4 3 2 1
First Edition

Random House Children's Books
supports the First Amendment and celebrates the right to read.

This book is dedicated
to middle schoolers everywhere.
This, too, shall pass.

# Contents

# A LETTER FROM THE EDITOR

*Dear Reader,*

*Middle school can be challenging, no doubt about it. It involves much more than moving to a bigger school with lots of new kids and a changing class schedule. It's about being literally in the middle—no longer a little kid and not yet a teenager. It's about finding your way through a whole lot of new experiences, and figuring out what you like to do, who your friends are, what you like to study, and, most important of all, who you are.*

*Writers can be awesome at helping us navigate our world, especially when things get difficult or confusing. At least, that's how it's always been for me. In this collection, thirteen of the best take on the challenges of the middle school years in all their complexity. With subjects ranging from loneliness, homework, changing classrooms, getting lost, changing for gym, school dances, cultural dislocation,* class trips, and family issues to the unexpected saving grace of music, art, friendship, and literature, this collection is intended to help you find your place in the middle of the middle school years.

In stories, texts, emails, formal letters, memoirs, poems, and even a short graphic novel, Totally Middle School *brings new perspective and reassurance, no matter your background, interests, or circumstances.*

*I don't envy you, making your way through middle school with your own set of challenges. But there are also some awesome opportunities in store for you. Though a lot of middle school was hard, I also recall it as the time when I began to come alive intellectually (reading! reading! more reading!) and emotionally (friends! friends! more friends!)—both of which are centrally important to my life now.*

*But whatever happens, it happens . . . and then it passes.* Everything passes. *Hopefully with some good times along the way . . . and some lessons learned. Perhaps this book will open up some doors for you. I really hope so.*

Betsy Groban
Cambridge, Massachusetts

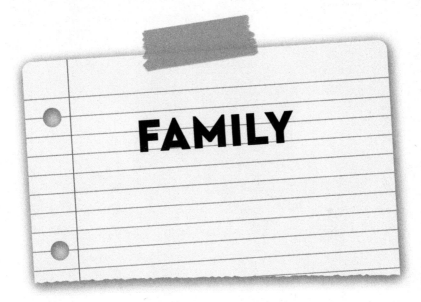

FAMILY

# Letters

## BY LOIS LOWRY

9 Cedar Circle
Cedar Harbor, Maine 04993

May 19, 2017

Ms. Margaret Metcalf
John Glenn Middle School
Cedar Harbor, Maine 04993

Dear Ms. Metcalf:

I have just been informed that you are to be my
English teacher when I enter Middle School next
year.

   As you can see, we learned in English this
past year how to write a Business Letter. This is
a Business Letter.

I understand that our class will be reading *To Kill a Mockingbird* in the fall semester. I don't mind reading the book but I thought I would let you know that I have seen the movie two times. Boo Radley is my favorite character because he is badly misunderstood. I myself am often misunderstood so I know what that is like. I was badly misunderstood last December at a family gathering and I feel it may have affected my entire personality although I doubt I will become a recluse like Boo. For one thing, no one is going to leave me a house where I can live in seclusion, except possibly a rich uncle, but it is unlikely.

I am looking forward to Middle School and I hope that we will establish a satisfactory relationship next year. This is my Closing Paragraph and in it I am supposed to request some kind of action. I would like to request that you pay careful attention to the other letter I am going to write to you. It will be a Friendly Letter.

Yours truly,
Katherine Metcalf Anderson
Student

• • •

May 19

Dear Aunt Maggie,

Okay, I confess, I freaked when I found out that you're going to be my English teacher next year. I am trying to figure out how to deal with it and I'm hoping you and I can agree on some things. Ground rules, I guess we could call them.

One, I am going to call you Ms. Metcalf in the classroom, NOT Aunt Maggie—no one will have a clue that you are my relative—and you should call me Katie the way all my other teachers do, not Cutie the way you call me at home, not *ever*. And also: Is there ever a time in school that you have to say kids' middle names? I don't think so. But just in case: it's okay if you have to use my initial, M, but pretend it stands for Mary or something. Madison would be okay, or Mackenzie. I like those. I just don't want anyone to know my middle name is Metcalf. I use it on Business Letters because it makes me look like a lawyer or something. But in real life, like in school, if people found out that information, they would figure out we are related and that you are my mom's older sister. If that happens, I am going to reveal how you bullied her throughout her early years. I mean it.

One time, in English class last year, for Creative Writing, we had to bring in old photographs from our past and write stories about them. It actually was a pretty fun assignment. I brought in a picture of Jake (Remember Jake? Our golden retriever?) and wrote about when he ran off and we didn't find him for three days, and it turned out he was over on the other side of town in someone's yard, and they hadn't even tried to find his owners even though he had a microchip. I think they were planning to keep him but we got him back and didn't call the police or anything. We found him because we put up posters with his picture and someone called us. Turned out they had seen him in the criminals' yard, it made a very good story because it had a lot of Rising Action and a Climax, but my teacher only gave me a B-minus because it lacked punctuation and had run-on sentences.

Anyway, the reason I mention it is in case you are planning an assignment where students bring in old photographs. Last year the teacher brought in some of her own, and in case you are thinking of doing the same, I want to be clear right now that the one you took of me that time when my diaper fell down and I was crying and had ice cream on my face? That one is off limits. You brought it out when we were at Grandma's house for the Fourth of July picnic, and everybody, INCLUDING BEN PRYOR, the next-door neighbor who is in tenth grade, looked at it and laughed—it was absolutely humiliating and is the reason I pretended to be sick when you had that get-together on Labor Day.

There are probably a lot of other photos that should be destroyed. Second-grade school photo, missing front teeth, horrible haircut, Tinker Bell T-shirt? Did my mom give you that one? Burn it immediately.

I have some questions about Middle School and maybe I should have put them in my Business Letter but too late, I've already printed that. My questions mostly have to do with changing classes. Is there a map or something? Do people ever get lost? I have a pretty crummy sense of direction as you well know from that time I told you in July that a left turn would take us to a place where we could buy fireworks, and then we went for many miles before I realized it should have been a *right* turn, and I know, I know, it was a problem that we had stopped for water at that little general store and then we had been drinking the water, and then we started telling jokes about Uncle Stanley, and well, you know what happened. The thing is, if you have to pee, you should not start laughing hard, it just doesn't work out well, and okay, it was because I said to turn left instead of right.

(And about Uncle Stanley. Actually, he is my one chance at someone leaving me a house where I can live in seclusion like Boo Radley, because Uncle Stanley is single and has no children and is pretty rich. But please do not ever mention him in school. You and I know what he does for a living but no one else needs to know that ever. Even if you just say the word quickly and go on to other things, well, someone might google *proctologist* and we do not want that to happen. Even if you and I know that he started from the bottom up, ha ha, now I am laughing again but luckily I am not drinking water.)

My main question is about getting lost in such a big school. Are the classrooms marked with numbers, and is there much time between classes, and are there restrooms, and oh please, tell me there is not a big discussion about gender because I don't understand any of that at *all*.

BUT DON'T DISCUSS IT IN CLASS. And especially don't say that I asked about it. You could maybe say "a student wondered. . . ." But then look around the room and do not focus your eyes on me.

Okay, about December, and Christmas.
Yes, I admit that I behaved badly, my mother
says I sulked—a word I hate: *sulked*. And I was
rude to you, I know that. The thing is: *You are
not supposed to give people underwear for
Christmas.* Not even expensive underwear, all
wrapped in beautiful paper with satin ribbon . . .
That actually makes it worse, because then
everyone notices the present and watches while
you unwrap it. Okay, I apologize. I should have
smiled and said thank you instead of slamming
the box closed and pretending it was meant for
someone else, and I should have come out of
my room eventually instead of staying there all
afternoon.

That has nothing to do with school, of course,
and I am really writing you a Friendly Letter
about school stuff. But it does make me think of
a question, which is: In Elementary School we
just went outside and played kickball and stuff,
we didn't really have anything called "Gym" but
I know they have "Gym" at Middle School, and I
am wondering if we are required to take off our
clothes and take showers. Probably teachers don't
have to. But students? Is that required? If it is, I
think it might be against the law. Or would there

be a way to get out of it? When I went to summer camp, my mom was willing to tell the camp nurse that I was allergic to several things. Liver, and cooked carrots. She lied on my behalf because I told her I wouldn't go if they made me eat those things. Maybe it would only qualify as a fib. But my mom was willing to do it, and she might be willing again, so I'm wondering if she could tell the school nurse that I have some disease that means I can't take showers, would that work, do you think?

And don't make any comments about my mom telling a lie. She and I both know that you smoked all through high school. And she never told on you but I could still rat you out to Grandma.

Just as a side question, and maybe you don't know the answer to this, but do all female Middle School students wear bras?

And while I am asking questions, does *To Kill a Mockingbird* have similes and metaphors? Just asking, no reason.

Love,
Your niece
(but under no circumstances
should anyone know that!)
Katie

• • •

John Glenn Middle School
Cedar Harbor, Maine 04993

May 22, 2017

Katherine Metcalf Anderson
9 Cedar Circle
Cedar Harbor, Maine 04993

Dear Ms. Anderson:

Thank you for your very interesting Business Letter, and the additional Friendly Letter that accompanied it.

Let me inform you that, just for the record, I smoked only during my last year of high school, and not the years preceding it, which you accused me of.[1] And I have not smoked since February 7, 2004. My sister, whom I believe you know well, continued smoking until 2005, thereby breaking an agreement we had made to stop together. (She thought I didn't know, but I borrowed a jacket from her that September, and it reeked of Marlboros.)

---

[1]   This should say "of which you accused me." But sometimes one makes exceptions.

You will probably not have any problem navigating the corridors of the middle school, unless, of course, you are still having trouble distinguishing left from right, which clearly gave you some difficulty that day last summer when we went to buy fireworks. The science lab (smells scientific, like alcohol) is on the right-hand side of the hall and the art studio (smells artsy, like turpentine) is on the left. At the other end of the hall, the music room (sounds squawky, like clarinets) is on the right, and the library (sounds hushed, like pages turning) on the left.

And you need not be concerned about restrooms. There are many, several on each floor, some marked GIRLS and some marked BOYS. They do not actually say that but use silhouettes, one with a skirt, one with trousers.

(I should mention, perhaps, that in my fifteen years of teaching at this school, I don't recall ever seeing a female student wearing a skirt. Still, everyone seems to accept that a picture of a skirt indicates a female person. Last year a seventh-grade boy found it amusing to wear a kilt. But it only lasted a day and he gave it up as a bad idea. I think the other boys gave him a hard time.)

And speaking of water: yes, there are showers at the middle school. It is not a big deal.

Sincerely,
Ms. Margaret Metcalf
Teacher

 **Lois Lowry** is the beloved author of many books for kids, including *The Giver* and *Number the Stars,* both of which won the Newbery Medal. Her books have won countless awards, and several have been made into movies and plays. Ms. Lowry was born in Hawaii and has lived all over the world. She spent her middle school years in a small town in Pennsylvania with her grandparents and many other relatives nearby. Her sister (who was clearly her mother's favorite) was three years older, and her brother (whom her dad liked best, no question) was six years younger. As a child her favorite activities were reading, writing, and drawing, and her mom always urged her to *go outside* and get some exercise! Her favorite food by far was cherry pie, which she was given every year, with candles, instead of a birthday cake.

She has three grown children and four grandchildren. None of them is her favorite. She currently lives with her Tibetan terrier Alfie in a farmhouse in Maine, surrounded by meadows and flower gardens.

# What Planet Are You From?

## BY GREGORY MAGUIRE

The girl seated on the front-porch swing looked up at the sound of a slamming screen door. She winced at the approach of the second girl, who was exactly the same age. The girl on the porch swing said, "I do declare, Beulah Mae, that the sunset on this Alabama bayou is a sight to see, or my name isn't Hannabelle Lee. It's sweeter than sweet pecan pie made with—"

"Extra sweetener?"

"Hush your mouth, darlin'. Never let evil mockery escape your lips. T'ain't ladylike."

"*You* shut up," replied her sister in a nice-enough tone of voice. "Margaret Mary Flynn, quit your stupid Hannabelle Lee routine. I have some breaking news, and it isn't good."

"I reckon I don't know what you might be talking

about, dear sister. This April sunset on the dear old Alabama bayou—"

"Stop it. *Stop* it. This is what comes from too much Civil War on Netflix. You don't even know if Alabama has a dear old bayou or a . . . a dear old . . . fjord. Or a bat cave. Or a divided highway. This is *important*, Midge."

The seated girl put down her invisible thread and the nonexistent embroidery hoop upon which she'd been pretending to stitch an improving sentiment, probably a Bible verse. "Sister, you are uncommonly, um, good at ruining the mood of an Alabama evening."

"It's half past eight in the morning. Midge, wait'll your sick noggin gets a load of this. I just heard Grandma yammering on the phone with one of her bingo friends."

Grandma Flynn was hard of hearing, so when she used the telephone, she talked loudly. No such thing as a secret when it came to Grandma Flynn. "Why, whatever did that sweet old lady let slip out of her sainted lips?"

"Margaret Mary, I'm about to smack you." Bridget Flynn folded her arms and glared at her twin sister. "If you don't drop the Southern belle act, I'll just keep the news to myself."

Margaret Mary sighed and fanned herself with an

invisible something or other. "Shall we take a stroll in this balmy evening and perhaps partake of a mint julep?"

"You thinking a Coolatta at Dunks? Sure." Sometimes getting Margaret Mary out of the house could jostle her into being slightly more normal.

Margaret Mary, who styled herself Hannabelle Lee, tried to link her arm with that of her twin as they set out to take the air. Bridget, who refused to be Beulah Mae to her sister's loopy alter ego, pulled away, saying, "Don't take your airs out on the street, Midge. That's the rule." Dunkin' Donuts was only around the corner, past Budget Tires and the dollar store, but after four minutes on the public sidewalks, people might stare. It had happened before.

"My, my. Oh, dearest sister, industry is surely a-flourishing in the Old South," said Margaret Mary as a rusty truck with Massachusetts plates tried to back up into the Dunkin' Donuts parking area, got stuck, and stopped cold. Perhaps the driver was considering abandoning the vehicle and just running away. As they paused to make sure they didn't get run over while the driver made up his mind, the girls could see Grandma Flynn. She had stumped onto their back porch and was hauling the laundry off the line. Though it was halfway through April, the weather forecasters were calling for possible snow by afternoon. The buds looked as if they were ready to keel over from the fear of a late frost. No stamina. So much for your balmy Alabama evening.

Bridget demanded, "Are you ready to listen?"

Margaret Mary, known to her classmates as Midge Flynn but to herself as Hannabelle Lee Robespierre, seemed a little pale. Going from a story person back to her real self took a while; she had to gulp a couple of times. She went faint, either actual or pretend. It was hard to tell. A Coolatta usually helped. "Yes, I suppose so, darlin'. Though I'm feeling mighty poorly at present."

They pushed on through. It was the Friday morning of school vacation week. The other people in Dunks were two small women hunched at a table in the corner and several old guys in baseball hats and nylon windcheaters. The fellows all had yellow-white hair and big bellies and loud voices. Their New England accents were anything but Alabamian. Each man sat at a different small table with his legs spread out, but the guys were all talking as if they were in some club together. It was mostly about car repair, though Bridget noticed there was only one car in the lot. These grandpas looked as if they were beyond driving, or couldn't afford the insurance. But okay, thought Bridget—their noise will drown out any drama that Midge might start.

Midge and Bridget got their drinks. Bridget paid. Midge sipped with great delicacy while Bridget slurped. They didn't talk for a while, just listened. The timid women in the corner were wordless, staring into their Styrofoam coffee cups. The geezers were talking at each other without really listening. (The way Midge did when she was being Hannabelle Lee.)

"I bring my car to Toyota? Oil change, seventy-eight dollars. I bring it over here? They charge you fifteen bucks to rotate your tires."

"There's a guy in Newry, he comes to your house, does it in half an hour."

"I got a guy in Rottsberg, does my brakes, costs me eighty, eighty-five tops."

"Yeah, Barry give you the same discount he git. I come out one morning, what the hell. Truck don't start. Battery kaput. 'What year is that junker?' he says. I tell him. Within forty-five minutes he there, man."

One of the old guys got up and left without saying goodbye. He had a limp and a cane. None of his buddies seemed to notice his departure. All this plate glass around boxy Dunks, all this wan, pre-storm light picking people out like specimens. The place was like a holding tank.

"I had a dead battery in the Ford, call up the guy. Comes full down the driveway, put those clamper things on—thirty-five bucks. I tell ya."

"Bridget?" Midge had rosier color, and her eyes weren't so wide-open, which were good signs. "Okay. Down to brass tacks. What's going on?"

Bridget Flynn knocked her straw around, making the last slush rustle in the plastic. Sounding like crinolines over tulle at a cotillion ball, maybe? "I heard Grandma on the phone telling someone they already sent out the middle school assignment letters."

Margaret Mary put her hands on the edge of the table and folded them together. "Shouldn't those letters come to us? We're the students."

"Who knows? Listen. It's bad. They don't want to send us both to Trenton." Trenton was the middle school nearer them, just the other side of Target.

"We're going to Lapham?" Margaret Mary shrugged. "Oh well. It's a longer bus ride, but everyone says the cafeteria is better. Not so dirty. Nicer side of town, I guess."

"No, you're not getting it, Midge. *One* of us is going to Trenton. The other to Lapham. I don't know who is where, but they're splitting us up."

Margaret Mary looked at Bridget. She didn't look all brave Scarlett O'Hara, just scared. They had been in school together for six years, eight if you counted preschool. Had sat next to each other, chosen each other for teams, dressed alike even at Halloween. They were so different, but their faces were the same. "But can they *do* this?"

"Well, they got two schools, don't they? Grandma was yelling into the phone that you can't—what's the word?—ask for a change. *Petition.* You can't petition for a change. The decision about which middle school kids get assigned to is always final."

That was how it had been presented to them a month ago by the school superintendent, who had broadcast his message over the murmur of the rising sixth graders in the auditorium. "You'll find yourselves in middle school with some of your grade-school friends and not with others," he had told them. "But you'll all come back together in the town's single high school, so deal with it." The applause had been vigorous and ironic, because almost everyone in fifth grade had someone they couldn't wait to get away from. You could always hope.

But Bridget and Midge! Midge—otherwise known as Margaret Mary Flynn, at one time Midge the Midget, sometimes Hannabelle Robespierre, less frequently Her Royal Highness Violetta Fiortini, late of the African Alps—Midge and Bridget had never been separated before.

Separated from each other, that is.

Separated from their mother, yes. She was in Taos or Denver. Or on the Gulf Coast—there'd been a glossy postcard, maybe of the Mississippi Delta or someplace. A lot of hanging ivy and Greek columns. She was finding herself. Twins had been one child too many; she couldn't deal.

Separated from their father, yes (everybody has a father, but he isn't always accounted for).

Separated from their grandmother—long-suffering Mrs. Flynn—rarely. Bingo nights were about it. Grandma Flynn was grim but constant about it; you had to give her that.

But separated from each other? Never.

"What are we going to do?" asked Margaret Mary in an uncommonly small and ordinary voice. She picked up someone else's crumbs with a wet finger and flicked them onto the floor.

Fifth graders couldn't budge a school official on a matter that defeated even parents and guardians. So Bridget shrugged. She didn't mean for it to come across as loose and casual as it must have looked. Margaret Mary got an expression on her face. *Here we go,* thought Bridget as Midge started right in.

"They think, dear sister Beulah Mae, we are going to *quail* and *shrink,* but we Alabama women are made

22

of sterner stuff," said Margaret Mary in her Hanna-belle Lee voice.

"Cut it out," muttered Bridget. "It doesn't work in the real world, Midge."

From a table two over: "Guy over to Lopers Falls, he'll forget to bill you the oil change once ya get him talking about the mess in Warshington, D.C. Course the oil he put in is dirtier than what he drain out."

Margaret Mary's voice was rising into that carrying falsetto. "We'll refuse to be parted. No force in nature can part us. The Union can split, but sisters, never." She gripped Bridget's forearm with a rather unladylike claw. "I tell you, sterner stuff, Beulah Mae!"

"Let's get out of here," said Bridget. "I can finish my Coolatta outside." She swept Margaret Mary's empty plastic cup into the bin and they turned toward the door.

The two birdlike women were trying to leave at the same time. One, Bridget now saw, was a put-upon younger woman with a serene expression. She sported a hairnet and a white jacket with pockets, like a nurse's aide. With one hand she was holding ajar the door to the vestibule and with her other hand she was en-couraging the older woman gently toward the strip of threshold.

The older woman was dreadfully thin. She held

her pipe-cleaner elbows tight to her waist. She wore a funny padded vest where a belt would go; it hung down from straps on her bony shoulders, like a crib bumper repurposed into a weird fashion accessory. Her hair was tortured gray straw, though her body didn't look so old. Her face was pinched and her feet scuffed and she looked at the floor. "Come on, this is the first one of two, Flossie. You can do it," said the healthier young woman. "We got in here, didn't we? We can get out. Lift your foot."

With effort, the starved-looking older woman managed to cross the threshold into the vestibule. There wasn't even a step, just a metal line flush in the floor. Once she'd done that, her other foot dragged along easily enough, and the pair of women made it swiftly to the edge of the second door, the one between the vestibule and the outside world. Some invisible force field intimidated the older lady. Who, Bridget realized, was probably more shattered than old and decrepit.

Bridget hung back and watched as the Flossie lady struggled to get herself over the second imaginary hurdle. Behind them, Margaret Mary muttered at dangerously increasing volume: "Our own dear *Papa,* if he was still with us, bless his heart, would take up his firearms to keep us together. Or hire us a tutor from Harvard or Princeton, one of those better Northern establishments. We could continue our learning in the comfort and safety of our own homestead. Genteel and protected. Why must we suffer?"

"Then there's the time where they forgit to bill me the timing belt and say it's my fault. I call the sheriff; I won't be pestered for repair bills I never get."

"Come on, Flossie. You can do this; you've had lots of practice today. Upsy-daisy. There we go."

Eager to evacuate Midge and her fancies, Bridget had shoved through the first door. Flossie, successfully outside now, shuffled toward the only car in the lot. "Why, dear sister, must we suffer?" bleated Margaret Mary, coming behind. Looking up at the caregiver, who had paused to keep the door open for the girls, Bridget found she couldn't speak. She just didn't know the answer to "Why must we suffer?" By the expression on the attendant's face, neither did she.

Bridget herself paused at the threshold to the parking lot, and then stepped over it. She held the door for her sister, but she didn't look back.

They turned the corner in silence. Shivering with the sharply dropping temperature, Grandma Flynn was planted on the front porch with her arms folded, waiting for them. A look of sour satisfaction toasted her red face. She could hardly wait for them to cross the street. "I got some news for you two, and no mistake," she bellowed. "I'm just off the line with the assistant superintendent of schools, no less."

Margaret Mary stepped off the curb first. Bridget lingered a moment. The truck finally lurching out of the parking lot at Dunks picked up speed and took a turn on two wheels, as if the driver meant to make up for lost time. It must have good clean motor oil in its metal veins and a new timing belt. It missed Margaret Mary entirely. The wind brushed Bridget on the face, but that was all that happened—it spared her, too, by a Confederate whisker.

Grandma Flynn was still there when the truck disappeared. She didn't even look anxious. She expected her granddaughters to live, for the love of Pete. She had gone to bat for them, after all. She had attempted something, and her old Irish face couldn't hide the satisfaction of having fought a good battle. But had she won? And if so, what was the outcome? *Had* she been arguing that the twins should be kept together?

Or maybe that they shouldn't?

Bridget wanted to stay with her sister and take care of her in the treachery of middle school. At the same time, she hoped the cause was lost, and that they would both have to be on their own at last.

Bridget was divided in half, twins in more ways than one.

The sisters still didn't cross the street. A car was

coming. As they waited, the wind off the Alabama bayou pushed the hair away from Margaret Mary's cheeks and brow. An identical wind, though hailing from central Massachusetts, worked its identical way through Bridget's hair. The car driven by the nurse's aide smoothed itself, as if every attempt was being made not to jostle the passenger. Brittle old Flossie sat stoically, looking ahead through the windshield, not able to imagine what difficult thresholds lay ahead, but probably worrying about them already. "Come on," said Bridget, "wherever we're going to, let's go."

 **Gregory Maguire** is the author of many books for kids and adults but is best known as the bestselling author of *Wicked: The Life and Times of the Wicked Witch of the West*. He was born and raised in a quiet neighborhood in Albany, New York, along with six siblings. His favorite activities were, and still are, writing, drawing, and reading. He was not a big fan of seventh and eighth grades, finding them a lot like elementary school but with rotating classrooms and more homework. However, after graduating from college, he returned to his former seventh- and eighth-grade classrooms as a teacher. During his one year of teaching, he took his students to New York City to see a play and *lost them all*, which helped him decide that being a middle school teacher was not in the cards for him.

A fun fact is that the play they saw was *Pippin,* with music and lyrics by Stephen Schwartz, who, twenty-five years later, would write the music and lyrics for the hit Broadway show *Wicked.* Gregory and his husband live in Concord, Massachusetts, with their three lively teenagers.

# When She Whined in Her Sleep

## BY GARY D. SCHMIDT

On my first day of eighth grade at Henry Wadsworth Longfellow Junior High School, Donny Lentz got the draft notice that told him to report to some camp down in Louisiana in two weeks. He would train for war for thirty days. After that, he'd be shipped to South Vietnam, where he would serve his country by joining the forces of the United States Army. *Congratulations,* the draft notice said.

It wasn't like he hadn't expected it. He'd graduated from high school in June and been bagging at the A&P ever since. He said he didn't want to start college and then have to leave, like his brother had already done.

I didn't know him all that well, since he was five years older than me and lived a couple of blocks away. We went to the same church, and if we saw each other there he'd nod or maybe wave or something like that, and then go on to his pew and sit a little apart from his parents, like he was leaving space for his missing brother. He was the only one in the church who didn't carry a Bible in with him, and I think that rankled Pastor Jamieson, since every so often he'd fuss about carrying your own KJV because you didn't want Jesus coming back and finding you with a crisp, brand-spanking-new Bible at home because that meant you hadn't been reading it and would you want to show an unread Bible to Jesus?

It must have been frustrating for him to see Donny walk in Sunday after Sunday, Bible-less. I wondered sometimes if that was why Donny did it.

I mostly knew Donny because he ran by our house every morning when I was leaving for third grade, then fourth grade, then fifth, sixth, seventh, and now eighth grade. He had this long, loping run, with his head back and his mouth mostly open, his toes pointed to where he was going, his arms low and working like loose pistons. It looked kind of dumb. But his dog made up for it. She was a border collie named Mindy, and she ran down the street like she was running the hills of Scotland, parting the high grass in front of her, searching for lost sheep, her lips pulled back and grinning, her ears back, her mouth open just a little, running beside

Donny so easily, every so often looking up at him to be sure he was okay, which he always was. She had two different-colored eyes—one blue and one brown—and when she pricked her ears up, the tip of the left one bent forward.

Usually Donny would just wave at me and keep on, but sometimes he'd stop, set his hands on his knees, breathe heavy, and ask how I was doing, how was school going, was I running because I looked like I'd be a good runner—stuff like that. Mindy would sit beside him, watching him close, waiting for the least sign that he was ready to go again. She wouldn't take her eyes off him, even when I rubbed the back of her neck or played with her tipped ear. She wouldn't take her eyes off him, even if I got down and scratched her chest.

On our street, I never saw Donny without Mindy. I think, if he could have, he would have brought her to church, too—which would really have gotten Pastor Jamieson going.

I knew Mr. Lentz, too, since he was the principal of Henry Wadsworth Longfellow Junior High School. I don't know what it was like for Donny to be a student in the same school where his father was principal, since he'd graduated before I got there. But maybe it was easy, since everyone liked Mr. Lentz. He went to every basketball game and soccer match and football game and volleyball match and track meet. And he went to every play the Longfellow Thespians put on, and every concert the seventh-grade choir, and eighth-grade choir, and ninth-grade women's chorale, and ninth-grade men's glee club put on. He knew our names, and sometimes he'd come and sit in the cafeteria with us— sometimes he'd even eat the food. And sometimes he'd come in and read to us, and he'd do all the voices. He was that kind of principal.

The Sunday after Donny got his draft notice, Pastor Jamieson began his announcements with the news. It seemed like he and God were all excited about it. Donny was being called to a Great Cause. He would be a small part in America's task of holding back Communist atheism. He would bear witness to the light through the strength of his arms. Then Pastor Jamieson went into an impromptu prayer. Like Joshua, may Donny Lentz defend his people. Like Samson, may Donny Lentz smite the godless. Like Gideon, may he lead others into battle for his Lord.

I don't know how Donny took all this, since it was prayer after all, and Pastor Jamieson was death on anyone who might look up for a glimpse, so we all kept our heads bowed and our eyes closed. I suppose.

But I don't think Mrs. Lentz was all that happy about the draft notice. She and Mr. Lentz left after the last verse of "Onward, Christian Soldiers" and weren't in the church vestibule when everyone was shaking Donny's hand and telling him he'd be fine and wouldn't it be good to see his brother again soon and Mr. Ingmer told him the joke about remembering which was his gun and which was his rifle and he'd better be careful with each one and the old guys laughed and Donny looked embarrassed and someone said he should remember to keep his head low and then no one was laughing.

I didn't see him and Mindy running the whole next week. I looked for them. But they never showed.

Until Saturday morning, when they came to my house and knocked on our door.

When I opened it, Donny was standing on the porch, Mindy sitting beside him, watching him with those eyes, her ears up and her left one tipped forward.

"Hey," he said.

"Hey," I said.

I told him congratulations.

"Yeah," he said.

I told him he must be pretty excited. I mean, going off to war. Fighting in the jungle. All that stuff.

"Yeah," he said.

"Killing commies," I said.

He looked at me. "Ethan," he said, "another way of saying that is 'Killing people.' "

I told him I knew that.

"A lot of people don't," he said. He reached down and played with Mindy's ears. "So," he said, "I have a favor to ask."

"Yeah?"

"I wonder if you'd take care of Mindy for me while I'm gone."

I looked down at Mindy. She was still staring at Donny with those eyes.

"Really?"

"Yeah, really. She needs someone to run with her, and play and stuff, and my folks aren't going to do that. I thought, maybe, you might like to."

That night at dinner, I asked my parents about Mindy. I said I'd take care of her all by myself. I said she wouldn't be any trouble. I said I'd run with her every day. I said it was, like, a patriotic duty.

I guess my mother thought so too. She started to cry, and left the table.

My father said I could take Mindy.

Donny brought her the morning he was going to leave for Louisiana. She was sitting beside him when I opened the front door. He had put a leash on her, and you could tell she didn't like it one bit. She held it in her back teeth, just beneath his hand, and every so often she'd tug at it.

But her eyes never left him.

"She's a good dog," Donny said.

"I know."

"And she's smart as anything. Whatever you say, she'll know what you mean."

"I know."

"And she's really well behaved—except she'll try to get up on your bed at night, but don't let her."

"Okay."

"She knows she shouldn't be up there, but she likes to curl up in the covers."

"All right."

"Don't let her."

"Okay."

He played with her ears.

"She loves peanut butter, so maybe give her a little every so often."

"I will."

"Okay."

"Okay. I'll take care of her, Donny."

"Okay." He handed me the leash, and immediately Mindy looked at me, her ears went down, she looked at Donny, she looked at me again, and she gave this small whine from deep inside her.

He played with her ears a little more; then he turned and walked down the porch stairs.

Mindy pulled once to follow him, but she knew. She lay down, put her head on her front paws, and watched him walk away.

That whole day, if she was outside, I had to keep her on the leash; otherwise she would have run back home. When she was inside the house, she lay by the front window, watching.

That night, she never even tried to jump up to my bed—even when I told her she could.

And I knew she was Donny's dog. I knew that. But somehow, it changed everything. Somehow, when you know you have a dog waiting for you to come back home, it sort of puts junior high in perspective. I mean, a dog doesn't care if you get first or second or third seat in band. A dog doesn't care if you can't spell *effacious,* or *efacacious,* or *efficacious,* or whatever. A dog doesn't care if Mr. Blue drives sixty miles an hour south while Mr. Green drives forty-five miles an hour north and how far apart are they after twenty minutes?

A dog is just waiting for you to come home and run.

I'm not sure Mr. Lentz cared all that much about Mr. Blue and Mr. Green, either, because whenever I saw him in the halls of Longfellow Junior High, he only asked about Mindy. "She behaving?" he'd ask.

"She's great," I'd say.

"We appreciate what you're doing," he'd say.

"Thanks," I'd say. "Tell Donny she's fine. How's he doing?"

Then Mr. Lentz would nod, and he'd give a little wave, and go to wherever junior high principals have to go.


For a while, Donny wrote letters back to the church, and Pastor Jamieson read them aloud during announcements, and then he would pray for Donny smiting the Communist peril, and he would pray for protection from the enemy, and he would pray that Donny would return to the church victorious when God's will had been done. And I would wonder if, back home, Mindy was sitting by the front window, watching, praying her own doggy prayers for Donny. I even wondered who God listened to more.

She never watched me like she watched Donny. She was always looking for him. We ran every morning, and she watched. We ran every afternoon after I got home from school, and she watched. We ran past Donny's house, and sometimes Mr. and Mrs. Lentz would be on the porch, like they were watching for us, and Mr. Lentz would give that little wave, and Mindy would run up on the porch and wag her whole hind end at them and ask if Donny was home yet, and they'd scratch her behind the ears, and she'd know, and come back to me to finish our run.

Mindy even watched when we turned on the six o'clock news and saw the pictures of the soldiers fighting in Vietnam and I learned, I learned, I learned that Pastor Jamieson didn't know what the hell he was talking about. Mindy and I would sit together, and I would hold her, and I hoped we wouldn't see Donny on the screen. Not with what was happening to them there. Sometimes my mother would get up suddenly and turn the news off. Sometimes my father would use words about President Johnson that I never heard him say anywhere else.

Then the letters from Donny stopped. Or at least, Pastor Jamieson stopped reading what they said. I wasn't sure which.

And so, a year went by, and who knew how many hours of algebra problems, and social studies essays on foreign cultures, and life science lab reports, and book evaluations on *To Kill a Mockingbird* and *1984* and *The Diary of Anne Frank* and *Flowers for Algernon*— all done in the dining room while Mindy watched at the front window. And who knew how many hours of running with Mindy—enough so that, late in the spring, when Mr. Lentz saw me run the mile in PE—he was the PE coach too—he told me I should run cross-country in ninth grade, and I told him I would.

At the beginning of my last year of junior high, two things happened. First, we stopped going to Pastor Jamieson's church. My mother said she'd had one too many "smites" preached at her. In the middle of a sermon about Jericho, she looked at me and she almost started to cry, and then she took my hand and she said to my father, "We're leaving." And we did. Right in the middle of the sermon, before the walls came tumbling down.

And second, Donny Lentz came home—but it was a few weeks before we found out.

I think Mindy knew before I did.

After a year, she had stopped looking out the front window—at least, she didn't do it all the time. Now she sat beside me at dinner. She lay beside my bed at night. She followed me to the backyard and caught anything I threw: a Frisbee, a tennis ball, a stick of wood, a biscuit. And I didn't need to keep her on a leash ever; when we ran, we ran just like she and Donny used to: side by side, with her looking up at me most of the time, and even sometimes jumping up and nipping at my butt, joking around like I was a sheep she was herding. Until one Saturday when she stopped when we got to the end of Donny's block, looked down it, and sprinted to his house. She wouldn't stop, no matter what I yelled. She ran down the street, scooted across the front yard like border collies do—close to the ground and fast—took the four steps on the porch with a jump, and skidded with her back legs splayed out to the front door.

So, I rang the doorbell. I mean, suppose she was right? But no one answered. Then I knocked because Mindy was watching and she wanted me to. But no lights came on—nothing. Even so, it took a long while before she'd come away—and after that, Mindy went back to watching out our front window.

She knew—but that wasn't how I found out that Donny was back.

I found out when Pastor Jamieson and Mr. Lentz knocked on our door one afternoon. I had just gotten back from school and was getting ready to run with Mindy. She was eager; she was standing up on her toes, the way border collies do. Ears up, left one tipped forward. Grinning. A perfect day: blue October, leaves starting to tilt toward new colors, high clouds, that dry smell of autumn. I was looking for my sweatshirt in the mudroom when I heard the knock, and Mindy scooted to the door.

Pastor Jamieson was in a full-on suit, of course. He wasn't holding his Bible, like he usually was, and he looked sort of stiff—maybe because we hadn't been coming since Jericho and things felt sort of awkward.

And I hadn't seen Mr. Lentz for a few days. Actually, when I thought of it, it had been a couple of weeks.

"Hello, Ethan," he said. "She behaving?"

"She's great," I said.

I looked at Pastor Jamieson. "Pastor, I'm sorry, but my parents aren't here."

He laughed a little. "You know, I've never done this before, but we're actually here to see her."

He pointed to Mindy.

"You're here to see Mindy?"

"Ethan, Donny is home," said Mr. Lentz.

And you know, I knew this day would come, but I suddenly felt like I was either going to throw up or cry. I mean, of course Mindy was Donny's dog. I knew that. Of course he was always going to come back and she'd be his dog again. Of course. But for the past year, we'd run together like we belonged together. And it didn't matter so much if during the day there were jerks who do what jerks do in junior high, or teachers who didn't like you because they were in a bad mood or because they hadn't had their morning coffee, or this girl who laughed when you asked if she might want to go out on Friday because there was this movie and you thought . . . but she never thought. None of that mattered so much, because Mindy was always ready to run.

I loved her.

"I think Donny needs his dog," Pastor Jamieson said.

"Ethan, at night, when he's alone, the dreams he has . . ." Mr. Lentz couldn't finish.

Mindy looked up at me.

I guess she knew.

"Okay," I said. I think that's what I said.

Mr. Lentz looked down at me. "I bet you meant the world to her this last year," he said. He reached down and rubbed her between the ears. "I bet this will be hard as hell for both of you."

I looked at him.

"I'm sorry," he said.

"It's okay," I said.

"No," said Mr. Lentz. "None of this is okay."


It was as hard as hell.

Mindy and I went for our run. It was longer than usual.

We messed around when we got home.

I took a long shower. I took a long time to get dressed. We played tug-of-war with my socks and I didn't try too hard to get them.

I found her leash and put it on—which she wasn't happy about.

She held the leash with her back teeth.

I tried not to cry as we walked the two blocks.

Then, as we got closer to Donny's house, Mindy dropped the leash, and she started pulling.

Then she was pulling really hard.

Then we were on the front porch, and she was wriggling so much, I could hardly take off the leash.

I rang the doorbell.

No one answered.

I knocked.

No one.

You can't believe how hard it is to get ready to give up what you love most in the world, and then not have anyone take it.

You can't believe how hard it is.

But then . . . then the door jerked open, and Donny stood there.

Mindy went crazy.

She jumped. She cried. She lay on her back with all four feet up. She whined. She jumped again. She ran around him. She nipped at his butt. She jumped again. She cried again.

And Donny, he never moved.

He never moved.

He looked at me like he didn't even know who I was.

He looked at me like I was standing way away on the horizon. A million miles away.

"Hey, Donny," I said.

He closed his eyes, and when he opened them, he said, "You shouldn't be here."

"What?"

But he didn't answer. At the sound of his voice, Mindy stood up on her hind legs and reached with her paws like she wanted to hug him, and with one quick move, he pulled back and smacked her on the side of her head, so hard that she yelped and skittered across the porch.

"Donny!" I said.

Mindy crouched into herself. She put her tail low between her legs, brought her head down, crawled back, and turned her belly up to him.

He kicked her square in the ribs.

I knelt down over her.

"It's Mindy. Donny, it's Mindy."

"Don't . . . No one can . . ." Then he closed the door.

I heard it lock.

And Mindy crept down the porch stairs, her tail still tight beneath her. Then she turned and waited for me.

I didn't need to put the leash on.

That night, and for many, many nights afterward,

Mindy slept on my bed, and when she whined in her dreams, I leaned over and held her tightly.

 **Gary D. Schmidt** is the award-winning author of many books for kids, including *Lizzie Bright and the Buckminster Boy*, *The Wednesday Wars*, *Okay for Now*, and *Orbiting Jupiter*. During his middle school years, he lived in Hicksville, New York, on Long Island, with one brother and an assortment of dogs, including Boots (a lovable mutt), Jiggs (a barking beagle), and Kim (a schnauzer). His favorite activity by far was visiting nearby Jones Beach, where he could swim in the Atlantic Ocean. He was also a prodigious reader and in middle school fell in love with the work of J.R.R. Tolkien, like most middle schoolers of his generation. He has lived for quite a while on a farm near Grand Rapids, Michigan—with dogs. He has six grown kids and two granddaughters. He divides his time between writing for kids and being an English professor at Calvin College, at Hamline University, and at the Robert A. Handlon Correctional Facility in Ionia, Michigan.

# Looking for Home

## BY KAREN CUSHMAN

### SECRETS

Mama and Daddy had a surprise.
I assumed they were not having another baby
because they were old.

And here was the secret plan
I was hearing whispers about:
*Don't tell Grandma and Grandpa*
*yet.*
*We are moving to a new place,*
*A place where it never snows,*
Said my daddy who had to shovel the snow.
*A place where oranges grow in the backyard*
*and roses in the front.*

*You can wear shorts all year round,*
said my mother who had to buckle us up inside
snowsuits.
Was this enough to make us leave
Chicago,
Sparkle the dog, and
Grandma and Grandpa?
Uncle Stooge and Uncle Chester?
Could they come with us? Will they at least visit?
Will there be whitefish and dumplings and Polish
   sausage,
Dressel's German Bakery,
and Marshall Fields Department Store, with the
fifty-foot Christmas tree?
Did they have lightning bugs
and summer rainstorms
and snow?
Was it real? Were we actually going to live
somewhere else?
Somewhere called California,
where everything was perfect
and dreams came true,
just like in the movies?

## TO CALIFORNIA

Someone was found to take Sparkle.
I hugged her, weeping
until her long cocker ears were wet.
Furniture was packed into a moving van.
Goodbyes were said.
I saw Grandma crying and I hugged her, too.
I was excited and scared and lonesome
already.
We started for California
on a snowy January morning.
Cocooned in the backseat of the car,
I vomited across the country
from Chicago to Los Angeles.
In Dallas, Texas, we stopped at a J. C. Penney
to replace the blankets, pillows, and towels I had
  ruined.
The J. C. Penney had a magic machine.
A clerk put our bill and our money
in what looked like a brass soup can,
which she dropped into a tube.
With a press of a button, the can shot up the tube
and across the ceiling to somewhere
in the depths of the store.
Soon with a whoosh it returned to us,

now containing our change.
If Texas was this modern, I thought,
what would California be like?
We climbed back into the car
where I was immediately sick
on the new towels.

# LOS ANGELES

With my frizzy perm and
little puff-sleeved cotton dresses
tied in the back with floppy bows,
and brown oxfords, sturdy and roomy enough
to last all year,
I arrived to find California girls
mature even in their
Catholic school uniforms.
California girls rolled skirts up shorter and
tucked matching blouses into tiny waists,
and tossed their hair in the boys' direction.
The nuns at my new school didn't like the way I
looked
or talked
or that the smartest girl in the class
had a whiff of
Polish and
Chicago about her.
*You might have crossed your Ts like that*
*in Chicago,*
the nun in my class told me with a sniff,
*but it is not proper here.*
And
*Those shoes might be worn*

*in Chicago*
*but they are not acceptable*
*uniform shoes*
*here.*
I went home each day
alone
to lie on my bed and
read.
In a book I could go wherever I wanted—
home to Chicago, to Grandma and Grandpa, or
over the ocean or
back in time and
imagine myself there.
I wrote letters to my grandma,
who couldn't read or write.
My grandpa wrote back,
enclosing a two-dollar bill each time,
so I knew he still bet on the horses,
for where else did one get
two-dollar bills?
Did he still drink Green Rivers at the drugstore?
Who was helping Grandma make *kolachke,*
sticking little fingers into the dough to make
dents for jelly?
Was Sparkle happy in her new home,
or was she sad and bedraggled,

her cocker ears hanging to the floor?
Did the neighborhood kids play
Red Light, Green Light without me?
Did they play hide-and-seek,
looking for
but never finding
me?

# GIRL SCOUTS

In Chicago I was a Brownie.
We wove potholders and made cookies,
sang and played games,
and told stories.
In Los Angeles I thought I'd join the Girl Scouts.
The California Girl Scouts
didn't dress in Girl Scout uniforms but wore
poodle skirts and
starched white blouses
and sleek black flats on their feet.
They didn't want to sing or play games.
They wanted to have parties
with boys
and dancing.
I sat alone,
my big brown oxfords tucked beneath my chair
so no one could see them,
until the meeting was over
and then my big brown oxfords
took me home.
I was not a California sort of Girl Scout.

# BECOMING CALIFORNIANS

My father loved California and the
heat.
He'd do cannonballs
into the neighbor's swimming pool
and float with only his nose,
his belly, and his toes
above the water.
My mother drank martinis
and served Thanksgiving and
Christmas dinner
on a picnic table in the backyard.
*Isn't this great?* she'd say,
over and over.
*It's warm enough to eat*
*Christmas dinner outside.*
I didn't think it was great.
Where was the snow?
And people with red cheeks
bundled up in scarves and mittens?
Where were
red cabbage with apples,
roast squab, and
lime Jell-O with whipped cream,
like at Grandma's?

My brother was as pale and thin
as a wisp of smoke
but he could run like the wind.
He found three boys his age
in our new neighborhood
and played basketball and baseball,
or just ran, fast as he could,
animated by youth and happiness
and friends.
I was by far the oldest girl
in our neighborhood,
blocks and blocks full of babies and
boys.
The girls at school talked about
bras and
boyfriends.
I had neither.
I was out of place, not good enough,
strange and foreign,
marked like the laundry my Irish mother
didn't get clean enough,
according to my grandma,
who hung it in the attic
so the neighbors couldn't see.
I wanted to go home.
My uncle Stooge raised homing pigeons,

which, taken far away,
still found their way back,
but not me.
Like a lightning bug in a jar,
flapping against the sides,
I was unable to fly free.
My mother said,
*You always have your nose in*
*a book.*
I did.
I found friends in books.
And hope.
So I read.
I was more lonely than anyone knew.
The loneliness came in flashes
but I swallowed it inside
and read.
Reading saved my life.

# GOING BACK

Three years later,
just before I started high school,
my brother and I took the train
from Los Angeles to
Chicago.
The Chicago air was heavy and steamy.
It made my hair limp
and my clothes sweaty.
People dressed funny
and talked funny.
We stayed at Grandma's house
but Grandma did not sleep
at the foot of my bed
to keep me safe,
as she used to,
but in her own bed
with Grandpa.
She did not say,
*I am so happy to see you again.*
Looking at my long legs and
wide shoulders,
she said,
*You are too big for a girl.*
She said,

*The fingernails you bite*
*collect in a sac in your stomach*
*and one day they will explode*
*and kill you.*
Grandpa did not play the spoons
anymore
or lead school children
safely across the street
anymore
or drink Green Rivers
anymore.
No one drank Green Rivers
anymore.
Uncle Stooge and Uncle Chester
stayed elsewhere so we could have their beds.
The house still smelled like pipe tobacco
but the uncles were not there.
Only the pigeons were the same.
Everything else was changed,
especially my brother
and me.
We were growing up
and away.
On the way back to Los Angeles,
the train broke down
and sat on the tracks for two days

in the middle of nowhere,
a place not Chicago
and not California.
Just like me—
not Chicago and
not California,
a too-big foot in each place
but at home in neither.
And I am not certain
if that is a bad thing or
a good thing.

 **Karen Cushman** is best known for writing historical fiction with gutsy girl protagonists, like *The Midwife's Apprentice*, which won a Newbery Medal, and *Catherine, Called Birdy*, which won a Newbery Honor Award. She was born in Chicago and moved to California when she was in middle school, with her younger brother. She read, wrote, and put on plays in her garage enthusiastically from a very young age, though she did not publish her first novel until she was nearly fifty. She lives on a soft green island near Seattle with her husband. She has one grown daughter.

# FRIENDS AND FITTING IN

# How to Make S'mores

## BY HENA KHAN

"It's almost time for our big adventure!" Ms. Wehrle drops a yellow paper on my desk.

I must be hearing wrong when she says our sixth-grade class is taking a three-day trip to "study science and nature, and things you can't learn in a classroom."

Three whole days? I took school trips at the La-hore Grammar School in Pakistan—my school until we moved to America this summer. But we visited places like Shalimar Gardens for a couple of hours. We didn't *sleep* there.

When I show my parents the yellow paper, they don't like the idea either.

"No, no, no." Abbu shakes his head. "I won't send my daughter into the jungle with strangers!"

Ammi agrees with Abbu, and I sigh with relief. It's

bad enough being stuck in middle school every day. It's taken me a month to stop getting lost in the giant building and find my locker. I'm finally beginning to understand how things work in America (HERE), compared to Pakistan (THERE).

THERE we stayed in one classroom all day
and teachers came to us. HERE we rush to
different rooms in crowded hallways before
a bell rings.

THERE everyone wore neat uniforms. HERE
kids wear whatever they want—even pants with
holes in them and numbered shirts.

THERE my school was all girls. HERE half the
students are boys—even tall and hairy ones.

THERE I had one English class, and the rest in
Urdu. HERE I think, write, and speak in English
all day long and go to a special English learning
class called ESL.

THERE I had my best friend, Deena. HERE
I have nobody to talk to, share secrets with,
or trade lunches with.

But just because I'm figuring it out doesn't mean I want to be alone *anywhere* without my family for three days. So I crumple up the yellow paper and throw it away.

A week later Ms. Wehrle calls me to her desk while everyone works on an assignment.

"Raniya, I don't have a permission slip for you for Outdoor Ed," she says, pointing to a pile of the yellow papers.

"Yes, ma . . . I'm not going." I stop in time before saying "madam," like I call my teachers THERE. It slipped out of my mouth during the first week of class and everyone giggled, including Ms. Wehrle.

"Why not? You're the only student not going." Ms. Wehrle frowns. "It's not just fun. There's so much hands-on learning about science and the environment, team building and more."

"My parents said I can't go," I say.

"Oh dear. Is it a matter of . . . finances?" Ms. Wehrle half whispers the last word.

"Pardon me?" I whisper back.

"If it's a matter of the cost . . . *ahem* . . . we can talk to the PTA and I'm sure—"

"No, thank you," I interrupt. My face grows warm and I look up to see if anyone is listening. THERE, Abbu used to have a job at an office where he wore fancy suits and shiny shoes. HERE, he goes to work in jeans and sneakers at a shop. But Abbu says we still have plenty of money.

"Well then, may I ask why? This is the only time in my twelve years here that any student hasn't gone."

"Oh . . . um . . . I don't know," I mumble. A boy named Tony with dark brown hair is definitely listening from his desk.

"Would it be okay if I called your parents to discuss it?" Ms. Wehrle asks.

"Yes. May I go back to my seat now?"

"Of course." Ms. Wehrle frowns again. As I walk past, Tony shrugs at me.

By the time I get off the bus and walk home, everything has changed.

"Your teacher called." My father is home. By "home" I mean the basement we are staying in for now that belongs to a nice old lady.

"Did you tell her I won't go?" I'm sure Abbu was as firm with Ms. Wehrle as he is with my sister, Soniya, and me.

"She told me about the learning that happens there that can't happen in a classroom. She said it's safe, and she will sleep in the same cabin as you—all girls. I told her thank you very much and gave you permission."

HERE I watch TV shows where kids roll their eyes at their parents and say things like "But, Dad," stretching out their words so it sounds like "Daaa-ad." I could never say that, even if I want to.

"Yes, Abbu" is all I say, although my heart is racing. Why didn't I tell Ms. Wehrle my parents don't speak English? At bedtime, I confess to my mother that I'm scared.

"You will be fine, *meri jaan*." Ammi always calls me her "heart." "Your teacher said it is most kids' favorite part of the year."

"It won't be for me."

"You always enjoy school outings." Ammi brushes my hair out of my face.

"That was THERE. Please don't make me go."

"Abbu told your teacher yes. We can't say no now. You will be fine." Ammi smiles. But I see the worry in her eyes.

There's a list of things we have to bring to Outdoor Ed. Abbu buys me a bright green sleeping sack from the home store. I pick out a hat and gloves. The list says "no electronics."

And now I'm sitting on the bus with my Outdoor Ed group, called the Frogs. I'm gripping my lunch as I sit on a hard green bench by the window, alone. It's louder than the school hallways as everyone talks in excited voices about what we're going to do at this place called Skycroft.

The bus pulls away from school, and Ammi shrinks into the distance. Just before she disappears from view, she wipes her eyes. She was quiet when she hugged me goodbye for an extra-long time.

As my chest tightens, I'm grateful she didn't cry in front of me. I would have crumbled into pieces, and Ms. Wehrle would have had to sweep me off the sidewalk. Ammi never cries. Even when we waved goodbye to our cousins and left our happy life THERE in Pakistan and everything I've known to board a plane HERE to Maryland three months ago, she forced a smile at me.

I take a deep breath and wipe my eyes. Three girls in sparkly T-shirts and fluffy boots are whispering in the seat across the aisle from me. Behind them, a couple of boys are yelling to others in the back of the bus. Another kid taps the edge of the window, like he's playing drums. I sink into my seat and wait for the hour-long ride to end.

*Screech.* I wake up when the bus stops. I look down at my lap and something is missing. My lunch bag! It's nowhere on the floor. Then I turn around and see Tony, in the bench behind me, holding my lunch and grinning.

My heart sinks into my stomach. I've seen bullies on TV, stealing lunches and shoving kids into lockers.

I don't know what to do, so I turn back around and say nothing.

"Don't you want this?" Tony asks, touching my arm. I tense but don't move. "I mean, what's left?" he adds. "I tried half your sandwich. Was that Sriracha mayo?"

I can't help turning around and staring at him. He *really* ate my lunch?

Tony smiles again.

"Just kidding. Here. It fell on the floor while you were snoring." He holds out the bag.

"Did I snore?" My face grows warm.

"Kidding. Relax. It's so loud on this bus I wouldn't know if you were. I can't believe they said no head-phones."

I don't have an answer, so I turn around again. This is the first time Tony or any boy at school has really talked to me. Spencer rides my bus and says hi some-times. He told me we missed the bus when it came early one day. Soniya called him my "friend" and Abbu quickly corrected her. "He's her *classmate*," he'd said.

"You forgot something." I feel a tap on my shoulder and turn. The lunch bag is waving in my face.

"Thanks." I grab it as someone gets on the bus. It's Heather, a counselor at Skycroft.

"Listen up, everyone. We're hiking for the next

69

hour. Leave your lunches in that bin and we'll bring them to the dining hall. Your bags will be brought to your cabins."

We file off the bus, and it's much colder than it was at home. As I slept, we traveled to a mountainous part of Maryland. Trees are everywhere, and the ground is covered in leaves. My hat and gloves are packed in my bag, so I shove my hands into my jacket and join the kids trailing Heather and Ms. Wehrle.

I look at the ground, trying to keep mud from getting on my white tennis shoes. A pair of red sneakers is staying near mine and I look up. It's Tony again.

"I was in ESL for a while too," he volunteers. "I'm from El Salvador. Where are you from?"

"Pakistan." I say it the way we do THERE, "Pock-iss-TAAN," and can tell he doesn't understand.

"PACK-iz-stan," I offer again, and now Tony nods.

"Right." He is quiet for a while, and I wonder if he knows anything about THERE. Abbu says most Americans have only heard bad things about our country, like the evil terrorists that made us leave. He thinks it's our job to tell people about all the beautiful things THERE, and what millions of real Muslims believe. But no one's ever asked me anything about that. I hope Tony doesn't either.

"Well, see you later." Tony catches up to another boy, who has blond hair. I'm suddenly warmer than before and glance around me. A girl from my math class is looking at me, and a little smile forms on her lips. Her name is Eva. I keep walking.

We finally get to the dining hall and I find my lunch and sit on a bench while Heather explains the rest of the day. Everyone groans when she says there's another hike and cheers about something called s'mores. Tony catches my eye from another bench as I bite into my sandwich. I can't help smiling, and hold out half in his direction. He smiles back, shakes his head, and takes a bite of his own.

"You have forty-five minutes to get organized in your bunks and rest," Heather announces.

I'm assigned to the Laurel Cabin, and my group heads along a path to a box-shaped building. Inside are a bunch of bunk beds, and everyone rushes to grab them. I start to worry that I'll be sharing with Ms. Wehrle, when I spot Eva alone next to a set of beds. I grab my bag from the pile and walk over to her.

"Can I share with you?" I ask.

"Sure. But can you take the top? I'm afraid of heights," she says.

"Okay."

"Nice sleeping bag." Eva points at her own, which is identical to mine.

"Yeah." I smile.

The other girls are chattering and some are changing

their clothes. I never change in front of anybody, even Ammi and Soniya. But HERE, we change our clothes for gym class every day. And girls undress in front of each other like it's no big deal. I've learned to change so fast, no one sees anything.

"You're in my math class," Eva continues. "You're new, right?"

"Yeah." I wait for her to ask me where I'm from, but she doesn't.

"I moved here from France in the middle of fifth grade," she continues.

"Really?" I'm surprised. Eva speaks just like the other kids.

"We lived in France for three years because my dad's in the navy. We move around a lot."

"Oh." That's why she doesn't sound French.

"You're lucky you started here in sixth grade."

"Lucky?"

"The end of fifth grade had parties and a promotion ceremony with a slide show. I wasn't in any of the pictures, and I didn't know anyone."

"I don't know anyone," I say.

"Yeah, but four elementary schools feed into our middle school. So everyone doesn't know some people."

"I guess." I don't see how that is the same as not having *any* friends, but I don't say so.

"I can't believe we have to go on another hike! I'm so tired." Eva rummages through her bag.

The second hike is better because I have my hat and gloves and Eva with me. Heather and Ms. Wehrle take us on a trail to the original Washington Monument. It's nothing like the tall, pointy white tower my family saw in Washington, D.C., the first week we arrived in America. This one is made of gray stones and looks like a giant barrel.

"What are s'mores?" I finally work up the nerve to ask Eva.

"Oh, you'll see." Eva smiles mysteriously.

After the hike, we return to the dining hall. The Frogs have dinner duty, so we have to set the tables. I see Tony walk into the dining hall with a bunch of boys. He grabs a handful of forks and drops them next to the plates I put down.

"Hey," he says.

"Hey," I answer.

Eva comes over and motions to me. "They want us to bring out the drinks."

I give Tony a half smile and as we walk away I can feel him watching us. Eva grips my arm.

"You like Tony," she says in a hushed voice.

"What?"

"I can tell. I think he likes you too."

"He found my lunch on the bus."

"I saw him talking to you before, and now he came right over to you."

It feels like Eva wants me to say something, but I don't know what it is.

"So?" She looks at me like we're sharing a secret, and I feel a pang of missing Deena.

"Yes?" I ask.

"Do you *like* him?"

"Yes. He's my classmate." I'm happy he didn't really eat my lunch and that he's being nice to me.

Eva tilts her head a little and looks at me like she's trying to decide something. Then she hands me a pitcher of water.

I learn what s'mores are after we eat cheeseburgers and fries. We go outside to a big fire and put big fluffy squares called marshmallows on long sticks to cook. They catch fire and we blow them out, and they turn black on the outside and gooey on the inside. Then we make a little sandwich with them on sweet crackers and pieces of chocolate.

Eva is sitting next to me and also talking to another girl named Laurie. Tony and his blond friend come over to us with a huge stack of s'mores on a paper plate.

"We're making a s'mores tower—the biggest ever. Wanna get in the Guinness Book?" Tony says.

"That's not very big." Eva looks unconvinced. "It's

like six s'mores stuck on each other. I bet the world-record s'mores are bigger than a car or something."

"That's why we need yours," Tony says.

Eva starts to hand him the squares she just finished assembling. Midway, she stops and shoves them into her mouth instead.

"Mmmm." She laughs as the marshmallow oozes through the sides.

"Fine!" Tony says. "Forget it. Let's just eat this thing."

We all tear into the s'mores tower, making it topple over and catching the pieces before they fall to the ground. My fingers are covered in melted chocolate and sticky marshmallow goo, but it's the best thing I've ever tasted in America.

"AHHH! SNAKE!" someone screams from the other side of the fire. Tony runs to see it while Eva, Laurie, and I run away and huddle near the door of the dining hall.

"Just a twig, people!" Heather holds up a small branch and throws it into the fire. "Relax!"

My heart still pounding, I tell Eva and Laurie about when Abbu picked up the hose in our garden THERE to water our jasmine bushes.

"It wasn't the hose! It was a long black snake," I say.

"Did it bite him?" Eva's eyes are huge.

"No. He dropped it and it slithered away."

"I would've died right there." Laurie shivers.

"Me too," I agree. This is the first thing I've told anyone HERE anything about my life THERE.

It's chilly outside, but it's nice by the fire, and with my classmates. I feel the warmth of the flames on my face, and in my insides. Tony is back on the other side of the circle now, but I feel him watching me. When I look back at him and our eyes meet, he smiles a little and then looks away.

At nine o'clock we head back to the cabins for bed. It's funny to see Ms. Wehrle in a robe and slippers, and everyone giggles. Ms. Wehrle does a little dance and turns around with her hands in the air and then she says, "Lights out, girls."

As I climb onto the top bunk and get into my sleeping bag, Eva settles into hers.

"That was pretty fun. Tomorrow we're playing Predator and Prey. And there's a reptile guy."

"Yeah, it was fun." I don't ask what a reptile guy is. I hope it's another good surprise. And that it has nothing to do with snakes.

"Good night, Raniya," she says.

"Good night, Eva."

We lie in our beds and the room falls quiet. Then someone sneezes really loudly and we all start giggling. Someone on the other side of the room snorts, and that makes us laugh even harder.

Suddenly I realize this is the first time I haven't kissed my parents goodnight. I say my prayers in my head and pause before I ask to go back THERE, to Pakistan—like I do every night. I still want to go back, but maybe not just yet.

And if we stay HERE, in Maryland, Outdoor Ed might end up being my favorite part of the year too. Maybe there are some things you can't learn in a classroom. Like how to make s'mores.

 **Hena Khan** is a Pakistani American writer who was born and raised in a quiet neighborhood outside Washington, D.C., with two younger brothers and an older sister. Like many writers, she grew up reading constantly and playing imagination games. Her unfulfilled desire for a pet (her parents didn't want animals in the house) compelled her to gather a huge collection of stuffed animals and to adopt furry caterpillars. She enjoys writing about her family's culture, as well as subjects ranging from spies to space travel. Hena lives in Maryland with her husband and two sons, less than two miles from where she grew up. "How to Make S'mores" is inspired by her own amazing Outdoor Ed experience, which back then was a full week of living in the jungle with strangers.

# The Skater

## BY MARY DOWNING HAHN

Cassie bent her head over the blank sheet of paper on her desk. After staring at it intently for several minutes, she removed the pencil from her mouth and wrote in large, strongly slanted letters, *On this, the first day of January, I, Cassandra Martin, resolve that I will never wear lipstick or nail polish. I will never cut my hair. I will ride my bike to school even if no one else does. I will climb trees and explore the woods. I will NEVER grow up.*

Cassie leaned back and scrutinized her New Year's resolutions. She nodded slowly. Thirteen was old enough—not that she meant to die before her fourteenth birthday, only that she'd stay as she was right now, the Cassie she'd always been.

Let her friends hang out in the drugstore choosing

lipstick and talking about boys and spending their baby-sitting money on fashion magazines. For some mysterious reason, they couldn't wait to grow up. Hadn't they ever noticed how boring adults were?

With a slightly smug smile on her face, Cassie slipped her resolutions into a folder marked *Personal*. Outside her bedroom window, the cold January sun touched the winter trees with bluish light. She still had time to ice-skate before dark.

Downstairs, her mother was sitting at the kitchen table talking to Mrs. O'Neil, one of those adults who had a knack for making Cassie uncomfortable.

Mrs. O'Neil watched her enter the kitchen. "You're taller every time I see you, Cassie. Does your mother feed you growing pills?" She smiled as if to say she was only joking.

Cassie recognized meanness when she heard it. Without returning the smile, she shrugged and reached for her jacket.

But Mrs. O'Neil wasn't finished. "Isn't it about time to get rid of those braids?" She tweaked one. "Julie has her hair done at Vera's Salon. Maybe your mom could take you there." Turning to Cassie's mother, she added, "Wouldn't she look darling with a perm and a nice cut?"

Cassie's mother sighed. "I've tried, but Cassie won't cut her hair until Ellie cuts hers."

"Ellie Boyd?" Ms. O'Neil sipped her coffee and frowned. "She's a strange one. Julie says—"

Cassie grabbed her skates. Julie hated Ellie and Cassie. And they hated her. Mrs. O'Neil probably thought she was just as strange as Ellie. Imagine, girls their age still wearing braids.

Interrupting Mrs. O'Neil, Cassie said, "I'm going skating, Mom."

"Have fun and be careful." Her mother sent Cassie an apologetic look to say she knew what was going on between her and Mrs. O'Neil.

Mrs. O'Neil refilled her cup and lit a cigarette. "You won't believe this, Loretta, but Julie told me . . ."

Cassie shut the kitchen door behind her. The air was so cold it almost took her breath away. She jumped over a frozen puddle and let the wind push her straight to Ellie's house.

Ellie had been sick a lot this year—bad colds, sinus infections, coughs. Sometimes Cassie wondered if Ellie was really sick or just didn't want to go to school.

At Ellie's house, Mrs. Boyd welcomed Cassie with a smile and a hug. "Ellie's upstairs in bed. She'd love some company."

"Is she still sick?"

Mrs. Boyd sighed. "Maybe you can persuade her to go skating with you. Fresh air would do her good."

"Cassie, is that you?" Ellie called. "I'm in bed. Come on up."

She found Ellie under a pile of blankets, reading. The bed was littered with comic books, scattered playing cards, used tissues, a Clue game, a checkerboard, and a spilled box of dominoes.

Ellie didn't look sick. She was no paler than usual. But when Cassie asked her how she felt, she coughed and said, "Not too good."

Cassie shifted her skates from her right shoulder to her left. "Do you feel well enough to go skating with me?"

"It's too cold out there." Ellie slid farther down on her spine. She coughed again. Harder this time.

"Lots of kids will be there. Arlene—"

"Arlene!" Ellie suddenly straightened. "Do you know what she wore to church last Sunday?"

Cassie shook her head. She went to Our Lady of Sorrows, but all the other girls went to the First Baptist on Main Street. How would she know what Arlene wore?

"Lipstick," Ellie continued. "She had on lipstick. And so did Julie and Janet and the rest of them. It looked like a lipstick club."

Cassie sat down at the foot of the bed and started an avalanche of dominoes. They clattered to the floor, but when she leaned down to pick them up, Ellie told her not to bother.

Ellie twirled a braid around her finger and scowled. "Julie gave me such a look—and then she whispered something to Janet. They stared at me and giggled."

"I hate Julie." If she'd been that mean to Cassie, Cassie would have run home in tears. "What did you do?"

"I told her she was a fat stuck-up snot."

"You said that in church?"

"Not *in* church, dummy. This was *after* church, when we were walking home."

Cassie felt stupid. Of course Ellie wouldn't have said that in church. To hide her embarrassment, she switched the subject back to Arlene. "Are you sure Arlene was wearing lipstick?" Just last week she and Arlene had agreed that only cheap girls wore lipstick. In fact, both of their mothers said they were too young to wear lipstick.

"Didn't I see her myself?" Ellie lay back on her heap of pillows and contemplated the bony hill of blankets covering her knees. "Next she'll be smoking cigarettes behind the gym."

The certainty in Ellie's voice irritated Cassie. "Arlene would never do that."

"She certainly smoked most of the cigarettes when we tried it last summer."

"Well, they were her mother's."

"The second pack was *my* mother's, and she smoked most of those, too."

The wind rattled the glass in the window and Cassie longed to be outside. She hadn't taken off her jacket, and Ellie's room was so warm she was perspiring. Soon it would be too late for skating. "So do you want to skate or not?"

"Good grief, Cassie, can't you see I'm sick? Do you want me to catch pneumonia?"

"I thought maybe you were just resting—"

"Maybe nothing." Ellie scowled. "Don't you care how I feel?"

"I just—"

"You just want to go skating with Arlene, that's what you want to do. Well, go on, what are you waiting for? Don't think about me lying here all alone."

Cassie toyed with the cover on her skate blade. "It will be dark soon, and—"

"We could have some hot chocolate, and I'll loan you my new Terhune dog story. You haven't read *Lochinvar Luck* yet. It's really, really good. The best one yet."

"I'll come see you tomorrow after school." Cassie felt guilty, but she wanted to feel the wind on her face and the ice under her skates.

"You like Arlene better than me," Ellie said. "You want to be just like her and wear lipstick and curl your hair and do all that dumb stuff."

"No, I just want to skate."

"Go, then. Have fun with Arlene. Don't think about me lying here too sick to go anywhere." Ellie coughed and reached for the glass of water on the bedside table.

Cassie couldn't stand another second of Ellie's whining, not with the sun shining, and the wind blowing, and the afternoon slipping away. "You know what I think? There's nothing wrong with you. You're a hypochondriac!"

Ellie threw the covers aside and jumped out of bed, her face flushed with anger. "What did you say?"

Cassie grabbed her skates and ran down the stairs. A handful of dominoes pelted her back. She silently thanked her English teacher for adding *hypochondriac* to her vocabulary.

Mrs. Boyd stuck her head out of the living room. "Are you leaving already?"

Cassie paused long enough to say "Ellie's too sick to go skating." Then she was out the door, in the fresh air, sailing on the wind. Free, free, free.

Cassie was so tired of the way Ellie acted. Throwing those dominoes was something a five-year-old would do. And that book by Albert Payson Terhune . . . Cassie was sick to death of dog stories. She didn't care if she never read *Lochinvar Luck*. She'd just begun *Wuthering Heights*. Heathcliff was a lot more interesting than a collie.

Let Ellie stay in bed. See if Cassie cared. She didn't

want to sit in that hot, stuffy room and drink cocoa and play checkers. Ellie always won, which made Cassie feel stupid.

At the pond, Cassie laced up her skates and looked around to see who was there. Little kids slid and stumbled and fell their way across the ice; groups of teenagers raced each other or played hockey; girls practiced spins and jumps. She glimpsed Arlene's red jacket in the crowd.

"Arlene!" she called.

Her cheeks pink from the cold, Arlene skated across the ice to meet her. "I went to your house, but your mother said you'd already left. Where've you been?"

"I went to see Ellie. She's sick."

Arlene shrugged. "She's always sick."

Cassie noticed a faint rim of red on Arlene's lower lip. "Are you wearing lipstick?"

"Julie let me use hers. We were experimenting with colors. This is Carmen Red—or it was, before it faded."

"But just last week, you said only cheap girls wear lipstick."

"Julie's not cheap and neither is Janet." Arlene looked closely at Cassie. "You should try it. Pink would look so good on you."

Cassie shook her head. She'd feel dumb wearing lipstick, like she was trying to be somebody she wasn't.

"There's Janet." Arlene took Cassie's arm and pulled her across the ice toward a group of girls. Julie was there too. Cassie hesitated. What if Julie treated her the way she'd treated Ellie?

Without warning, Arlene stopped so fast Cassie almost fell down. She pointed to a boy speeding across the ice with a group of hockey players. "There's Billy. Isn't he cute?"

Cassie looked at her. "Are you crazy? What's cute about Billy Travers?"

Arlene spun around in a circle. Her face had a strange, dreamy look. "Oh, just everything. His hair, his eyes, the way he smiles. He's so—"

"Short," Cassie interrupted.

"He's taller than I am."

"Well, he's shorter than I am."

Arlene and Cassie started laughing like that was the funniest thing in the world. Before Cassie could catch herself, her skates slipped out from under her and down she went. Arlene fell too. They lay on the ice and giggled.

Suddenly Billy Travers was there, hockey stick in his hand, staring down at them. "Are you girls okay?"

Arlene's face turned red and she struggled to get up. But her skates slid out from under her and she sprawled on the ice like a newborn baby horse.

Billy held out his hockey stick. "Lean on this," he told Arlene.

Still giggling, Arlene let Billy help her. Cassie got to her feet by herself.

"What's so funny?" Billy asked. "You guys were laughing like lunatics."

"Nothing." The girls started laughing again. They couldn't help it. Nothing was funny. Everything was funny.

Billy looked puzzled. "You're both crazy."

They laughed harder. Cassie felt like the fun-house lady who stood at the entrance and laughed and laughed and laughed and couldn't stop.

David Miller skated over. "Come on, Billy. You're holding up the game."

"Take it easy, girls," Billy said.

They watched the boys skate away to join their friends. Their voices rang across the ice. Their hockey sticks banged against each other.

Arlene groaned. "Oh, I feel so stupid. Why did I laugh like that? Now Billy thinks I'm crazy."

"Why do you care what Billy Travers thinks? He's pretty goofy himself."

"Billy's not goofy. He's the nicest boy in school and I really, really like him."

"You like Billy?"

"Everybody likes him. I want to ask him to the Sweetheart Dance before Julie does, but I'm scared he'll say no."

Arlene babbled on about Billy, but Cassie had stopped listening. Boys, dances—she didn't know what to say. She skated backward, a foot or so away from Arlene. The sun was low now, and the sky was red behind the bare trees. Soon the streetlights would come on, and they'd have to go home.

Turning to Arlene, Cassie yelled, "Race you across the pond!" Her skates bit into the ice and she sped past the boys playing hockey. She reached the other side well ahead of Arlene. Arlene said Cassie won because her legs were longer. They raced again and this time Arlene won. Cassie said it was because Arlene's legs were shorter.

They laughed and Cassie relaxed. Things were all right between them again. They practiced skating backward and spinning. Arlene did a series of figure eights, and Cassie followed her tracks in the ice.

The wind picked up, and the color in the sky faded. Most of the skaters had already left, even the boys.

With their skates over their shoulders, they ran down Forty-Second Street. In front of Arlene's house, they stopped under a streetlight.

"I have this great idea," Arlene said. "I'll ask Billy to

the Sweetheart Dance if you ask David—he's definitely taller than you. And we'd go together, all four of us."

Cassie stared at Arlene in surprise. "Are you kidding? David wouldn't go anywhere with me. I don't know how to dance or anything."

"I can teach you. It's easy. Barbara and Carol and I practice at Barbara's house. Her big sister showed us how to slow dance and jitterbug. It's really fun." Arlene took Cassie's hand and twirled around as if to prove how easy it was.

Embarrassed, Cassie snatched her hand away. "I'd better go home. My mother will think I've been kidnapped or something."

"Wait a second." Arlene grabbed Cassie's sleeve. "I have to tell you something."

"What?"

Arlene hesitated. "Don't get mad, but Julie and some other girls were talking about Ellie after church. Nobody likes her. If you stay friends with her—"

The good feeling from skating disappeared. "If I stay friends with Ellie, nobody will like me, either? Is that what you're saying?"

"I'm just saying you shouldn't do everything she tells you to do. You dress like her, you walk like her, you wear your hair in braids like her. You're not in grade school anymore, Cassie."

Cassie got mad then. She'd had enough criticism for one day. "Why don't you just shut up and mind your own business?"

"Why don't you?" Arlene ran up her front steps. The door banged behind her.

Cassie stood under the streetlight and stared at Arlene's house. What was the matter with her? First she and Ellie quarreled. Now she and Arlene had quarreled. Ellie didn't like Arlene and Arlene didn't like Ellie. At the moment, Cassie didn't like either one of them.

It was colder now, and she huddled inside her jacket. The wind pummeled at her back and pushed her forward. She didn't feel like flying or jumping. Trees groaned and branches rattled. She slipped on a patch of ice and almost fell.

Lights shone from the windows of houses. Sometimes the curtains were open and she glimpsed little scenes, like one-act plays. Families gathered around dinner tables; a man watched television; a woman stirred a pot on a stove; a boy opened a door and let a cat inside.

Cassie felt a loneliness she'd never experienced. She was alone, disconnected, outside in the cold and the dark. It was as if she were skating across the pond, but she didn't know how thin the ice was. The black water beneath her was deep. At any second she might plunge into it. She imagined swimming beneath the ice, trying to break it with her fists.

A car passed, its headlights swept her face, and she was frightened. She began to run, helped once more by the wind behind her. There, just ahead, was her house. Her father stood on the porch.

"Cassie!" He ran down the steps toward her. "Where have you been? I was about to start looking for you."

She pressed her face against his wool plaid shirt. It smelled of woodsmoke. She was safe now. She was home.

Her mother came to the door and hugged her. "You worried us. We thought you'd fallen through the ice."

"I'm sorry," Cassie said. "I didn't realize how late it was." She took off her jacket and hung it on a hook by the door. She hung her skates there too. Then, for a moment, she stood still and breathed in the comforting smell of warm food.

"Cassie," her mother called, "dinner's on the table."

She took her seat. Her mother sat at one end of the table and her father at the other. He cut the beef, and her mother served mashed potatoes and peas, still steaming from the stove.

A painting of a lake hung on the wall across from her. It had been there for as long as she could remember, peaceful and still, the sky blue, the water blue. In the corner, the china cabinet's glass door reflected the room. If she opened the door, she'd smell the pound cake her mother kept there.

Through the double windows behind her father, she saw the Jenkinses' house. In the kitchen at her mother's back, the refrigerator hummed. The television had been left on. Its screen cast a flickering light in the living room.

Everything was exactly the same as it had been, dinner after dinner after dinner—meat, potatoes, and a vegetable.

Deaf to her parents' conversation, Cassie ate silently. She imagined a time when her mother and father would sit at the table alone. Everything in the house would be as it was now.

Except Cassie. She'd be grown up, away at college maybe, but not here with her parents. Her chair would be empty.

She felt close to tears. Someday different people would live in this house. They'd fill the rooms with their furniture. They'd repaint the walls. They'd hang their own pictures.

Her mother and father would be gone. The house would no longer be her home.

"You're so quiet, Cassie." Her mother leaned toward her. "You're not crying, are you?"

"No, of course not." She pushed her chair away from the table. "May I be excused?"

Her father looked at her. "Your mother baked apple pie, your favorite."

"Maybe I'll have some later."

"I hope you haven't caught something from Ellie," her mother said.

Their worry followed her upstairs. Maybe she *had* caught something from Ellie. Not a cold or a cough, but something she couldn't explain.

Being Ellie's friend had gotten so hard. Maybe too hard. If she stayed friends with Ellie, she'd have no one else. Just Ellie.

But if she was Arlene's friend, maybe she'd have other friends—Janet and Barbara and Carol. But not Julie. Julie would never like her.

Cassie examined her face in the mirror over her bureau. Freckles, a pimple on her cheek, that bump on her nose she hated so much. Eyes too small. Mouth too big. Definitely not pretty or cute.

Who was she? What did she want? In elementary school she'd never asked herself questions like that. Then, she had been Cassie Martin, ten years old, bad at sports and math, good at art and reading. A bike rider, a tree climber, a skater, a creek wader, a daydreamer. She ran with a gang: Ellie, Arlene, Janet, Barbara, Carol. They quarreled and made up; they had fun.

She looked in the mirror for that Cassie, but all she saw was her thirteen-year-old self looking back at her.

Cassie picked up a pair of scissors lying on her desk. She lifted one braid and considered its weight and thickness. Suppose she cut it off? Suppose she cut them both off? Right now. This very night. Would she look better? Or worse?

She laid the scissors down. No, not now. Not tonight. Maybe another time.

She slid under the covers and opened *Wuthering Heights*. Outside, the wind murmured and howled. A draft of cold air sneaked under the windowpanes.

Tomorrow she'd call Arlene and apologize for shouting at her. They'd go to the pond and skate. She wouldn't go to Ellie's house. Like her mother said, Ellie might have something contagious.

**Mary Downing Hahn** is best known as the author of bestselling ghost stories and mysteries for kids, including *Wait Till Helen Comes* and *The Old Willis Place*. During her middle school years, she lived in a small house in Maryland with her younger sister and much younger brother. After years of begging, she persuaded her father to let her have a cat and, after even more begging, a dog. She was often in trouble for daydreaming, not paying attention, not following directions, and being sloppy and careless. Reading, writing, and drawing were her top skills, but she often got in trouble for doing those when she was supposed to be doing something else. She did not excel at math or team sports, but she did have a long list of nicknames, including Stretch, Spider, and Shorty. She lives in Maryland, the state where she was born and raised and the setting of many of her books. She has two grown daughters.

# Imaginary Mambo

## BY MARGARITA ENGLE

I sort of know how to dance,
so moves aren't the challenge
that scares me.
It's that partner thing—
waiting to be chosen,
standing alone
on the sidelines
with my nervous mind
and nerdy glasses.
I've seen enough PG-13 movies to know
that contact lenses, cool clothes, a sassy attitude,
and clipped-short
blond hair
always
work like magic,

attracting the perfect
no-losers-allowed
hot football player
who somehow boasts
both muscles
and brains.
Well, guess what—I'm not blond,
my idea of *fútbol* is soccer,
and I can't actually dance
even half as well
as the rest
of my family.
My parents and never-nervous
party-girl *primas*/cousins
were all made on the dance-crazy
island of Cuba,
while I was born here,
far from all those legendary drummers
who pound out exhilarating beats
on every street corner
in La Habana.
Whenever I have to perform my own shy
sort-of-dancy thing
at family gatherings—birthdays,
*quinceañeras,* and wedding receptions—
I'm never as relaxed as when I'm alone

in front of a mirror, with nothing
but music,
my heartbeat,
and any one of a thousand imaginary boys
I know how to invent.
They're all experts, smart but cute too,
and most importantly, easy to follow
as they lead, spinning me all over
our imaginary
dance floor.
If only
one of those boys existed!
I'd take him to next week's
dreaded
dreadful
deadline-looming
first-in-my-lifetime
Middle School
Mixer.
Why does the year's first dance
have to be called something silly?
It's still September—they could have waited
for Halloween so we'd all be protected from
   ridicule,
our embarrassed faces hidden
behind hideous masks

or hilarious ones.
We'd also know each other better by then.
We're not the same people we were in sixth grade,
so it's like meeting for the first time.
Everyone has changed in so many ways.
Hair, clothes, attitudes, and groups—old friends
tossed aside, new ones shown off
like prized possessions.
So what can I do?
Who will I dance with at a mixer,
whatever that means?

One week to go.
Seven days.
One hundred sixty-eight hours.
Ten thousand eighty minutes.
Six hundred four thousand eight hundred
endless
agonizing
seconds.
Should I get sick, skip the dance,
delay this ordeal until
Winter Formal . . .
or practice with my *primas,* get lessons from Mami
    and Papi,
maybe steal a boat and row to the island, where
    relatives

I've never met
will probably be eager
to teach me?
But what if they just make fun of me, Cuban-style,
by giving me a nickname that sticks forever,
something clever that means "dorky," "clumsy,"
"awkward," "klutzy," or worst of all: "wannabe."
Cubans and Cuban Americans don't live on the
   same planet.
Islanders are born dancing, while here we grow up
   watching TV,
playing video games, staring at screens, instead of
   talking
to living,
breathing
people.

With one week to go before YOUR first mixer
what would YOU do?
Run away from home?
It's a possibility, but the truth is I'm chicken.
Out there on the streets of Los Angeles, every
   stranger
is scary.

SEVEN DAYS TO GO!

One week of waiting to be humiliated
and I still don't have a plan
for this space-age countdown
to liftoff
or
for
an
explosion.

SIX MORE DAYS NOW.

The morning is warm and smoggy.
All the overwhelming hours at school
seem impossible, but somehow, I get through
the shame of sitting alone at lunch,
and by the time I go to my aunt's house
in the evening, dancing with my cousins
seems so intimidating that I secretly grow
anxious
dizzy
delirious
with fear.
So I SIT DOWN and pretend to be lazy,
hoping I won't faint and end up with broken bones

a concussion
or crushed
wishes.

FIVE DAYS.

I don't even try.

FOUR DAYS.

Is there any way to slow
a spaceship's countdown,
maybe use half days or tenths of days,
or substitute some other culture's unfamiliar
calendar?

THREE DAYS.

Is it possible to dance with my eyes closed?
No.
What about pretending the dog is my partner
and trying to follow four-footed steps instead of
   two?
Pretty funny, but not really useful
unless I want to dance

in a circus
or a zoo.

## ONLY TWO MORE DAYS!

The connection to my arms and legs
shuts down, as if someone has switched off
all the lights in the entire world.
So I give up, and go to the nursing home
to visit Abuela, because she suffered a stroke
not very long ago, and she still needs lots of
   company
to keep her connected to her own arms and legs.
It's in the brain, she explains as we stand side by
   side
in front of a physical therapy clinic mirror
while she practices
her balancing
exercises,
perched on one foot
like a flamingo.
It's not easy!
I almost fall.
Try it.
You'll see.
Standing on one leg

for more than a few seconds
is tricky.
Abuela needs to learn how to walk again,
because the stroke made her brain forget
where her feet are located in space,
so she gazes downward as she recites
heel, toe, heel, toe, reminding herself
to do first things first, placing one heel
on the floor, then slowly, carefully
lowering those toes.
Afterward, we talk.
The blood clot in her brain took away English,
so we're limited to her first language, but I manage
to tell her with *español* and gestures just how
   worried I am
about the mixer—a word I translate as *mezcladora,*
one of those big trucks that stir up wet stuff and
   gravel
to make hard, gray concrete, like a roadway
leading into the unknown.
*¡Ay, cómo me encantaba bailar!* my grandma says
with a sigh—Oh, how dancing enchanted me!
I smile for the first time in days.
It's so easy to be poetic in Spanish.
Her memories seem to float in the air like feathers.
If only I could feel that weightless

and graceful.

*No es fácil,* she says—It's not easy.
That's the only phrase any Cuban ever uses
when faced with a problem, and even though
the words might sound pessimistic, it's really
so much more hopeful than claiming that a goal
is impossible.
She leans on her walker as we stroll down a
  hallway,
gazing out windows at a garden with a fountain.
All in the brain.
Not easy, but possible.
I need practical advice.
All I have so far is fragments.
You have to practice, Abuela tells me,
adding, so that *you* can teach *me,* because I'm sure
I've forgotten.
How could my grandma forget her dance moves?
She's always been able to do the best rumba, conga,
or mambo at any party.
That night, when I go home,
I stand in front of my mirror,
wondering how I'll get through
tomorrow.

# DANCE DAY!

The mixer is after school,
so first I have to endure
one class after another,
feeling glad that I argued
with Mami and wore
jeans and a T-shirt
instead of a dress,
because guess what—
everyone else is wearing
regular clothes too.

The gym looks huge, even though
it's the same size
as always.
A table with punch and cookies.
Balloons on strings, drifting toward the ceiling.
Boys stand around in clusters, while girls
jump up and down, wave their arms, and giggle,
until finally, someone I recognize
from math class
pulls me into the girl crowd, where I hop
like a three-year-old, suddenly feeling exhilarated,
relieved to discover that no one else knows
paired-up-partner steps,

so there's no pressure
to follow
a sweaty
boy.
Later, when boys start to join in,
my apprehension returns, but at least
it's not real horror anymore,
just his right hand on my waist,
my left hand on his shoulder,
and our other fingers
clasped
in air.
He's nothing like the thousand boys
I've imagined.
Just a shy kid who looks worried
as he watches his feet.
We do a little shuffling thing,
pretending we know where we're going
until the slow music ends and everyone
goes back to jumping around in time to a fast song,
having fun, laughing, maybe even secretly
   imagining
that we're good at this, experts like Abuela
in her memory,
floating
and feathery,

our minds filled
with *no es fácil*—it's not easy
possibilities.

ONE WEEK AFTER DANCE DAY.

Okay, so I didn't end up with a boyfriend
or dance skills,
but now I hang out with the girl
from math class, and at lunchtime
we eat in a crowd of proud nerds,
and starting tomorrow, I plan to practice
walking, talking Spanglish, and dancing
to old Cuban music
with my lonely grandma.
The thing about new possibilities is:
it feels so good to share them.

 **Margarita Engle,** recently named the Young People's Poet Laureate by the Poetry Foundation, is a Cuban American poet, novelist, and journalist. She won the first Newbery Honor Award ever awarded to a Latina writer, for *The Surrender Tree: Poems of Cuba's Struggle for Freedom.* When in elementary school,

she lived in Los Angeles and frequently visited extended family in Cuba. She and her sister surrounded themselves with dogs, cats, rabbits, and wildlife, including lizards, frogs, fish, turtles, and an injured mud hen. Her sister had a seven-foot boa constrictor that she wore around her neck like a scarf. Her favorite foods were dulce de leche candy and coffee ice cream, and her favorite activities were reading adventure stories and writing poetry. By the time Margarita was a teenager, the United States no longer allowed travel to Cuba, and she felt a terrible sense of loss. Now, most of her writing is in verse and reflects both her Cuban heritage and her love of nature. She lives in central California with her husband, and when she's not writing, she volunteers at a wilderness search-and-rescue dog-training program. She has two grown children and four grandchildren.

# FINDING YOURSELF

# Ode to the Band Room

## BY JOYCE SIDMAN

Before class, it sits quietly
waiting.

Just some scattered chairs,
smudged song sheets,
and the tilted skeletons
of music stands.
A faint odor of metal and spit.

Soon, though,
it fills with our jokes and jostling.
Instruments burst from their pebbled black cases
in a chatter of snaps.
We find our chairs:
the willowy clarinets, wistful oboes,
blaring trumpets, and slick trombones;

the growly saxophones
and the distant, formal French horns.

We riff through scales and tricky phrases
and shuffle our scores.
Then

the baton lifts,

and like a giant organism with many moving parts,
glinting and wobbling,
we gather our collective breath
and *b l o w*.
Letting loose with abandon,
knowing these walls
were built
for NOISE.

 Award-winning poet **Joyce Sidman** was inspired to write this poem by her son's happy experience with his middle school band. She is the author of many books of poetry for kids, including the Newbery Honor winner *Dark Emperor and Other Poems of the Night*, and is a recipient of the prestigious NCTE Award for Excel-

lence in Poetry for Children. She grew up in Connecticut in the hippie era as the middle sister of three girls (all girls all the time!). Her family had a dog—a German shepherd—and various other pets that her sister adopted over the years: a crow, a tortoise, an iguana. She was a voracious reader and always kept a journal, which helped her decode the worlds of school and relationships. She discovered poetry in high school, encouraged by a sympathetic teacher. A firm believer in "pondering time," especially for kids, she lives with her husband and their dog, Watson, near a large woodland in Wayzata, Minnesota. She has two grown sons.

# TBH I Need HELP!! 🙈

## BY KATHERINE PATERSON
## AND JORDAN PATERSON

### [TEXT]

**Amanda (to older cousin Katie):** Hey Katie.
How are you?
**Katie:** Hey Amanda! I miss you, whatup??
**Amanda:** I need advice. A LOT OF ADVICE
**Katie:** Let's FaceTime.
**Amanda:** Yes! 🖤

### [FACETIME]

**Katie:** So what's happening? I miss you since your
family moved away.
**Amanda:** Oh, Katie, I miss you too. I'm starting
middle school next week and *everything* is

freaking me out. I just saw *Middle School: The Worst Year of My Life* and I'm worried that my middle school will be like the school in the movie, with an evil principal and endless rules that make no sense. I know that the movie was made-up and exaggerated, but even if it's a little tiny bit true, *eeeeek!*

**Katie:** First off, relax! That movie was totally *fiction.* I wish we lived closer and I wasn't mucho busy so I could visit Elm Street Middle and *assure* you that it will be nothing like your nightmare scenario. Would it bum you out to know that I loved middle school? Okay, I won't say it, but I really did.

**Amanda:** Did you honestly love middle school? From the first day?

**Katie:** It's really not as scary as you think!

**Amanda:** But last year we went to a concert there and I got lost trying to find the girls' room. I thought I'd never see my parents again.

**Katie:** Oh, my poor cuz, didn't they give you a map of the building at orientation?

**Amanda:** Yes, they did pass out maps. But I've never been good at reading maps. And it's not just the building, it's all the kids. ESMS has over three hundred students in each grade. I'm not good at math, but even I know that three hundred in each year adds up to nearly one thousand kids.

Katie: It's too early to be overwhelmed. Take a deep breath. Enjoy your weekend. Just figure that on Tuesday those other two hundred ninety-nine kids will be new too. A lot of them will be getting lost right along with you.

Amanda: Thanks. Okay. Okay. I'm taking a deep breath. Tomorrow is the day. Wish me luck.

Katie: Of course! Good luck!

Amanda: Wait! I nearly forgot! One more thing. *Lockers!* Do you remember Sean? My nerd neighbor who had a crush on you when you visited last summer? He said that lockers will do me in. I'll forget my combination, forget where it is, forget which book or notebook I need . . . well, basically *everything*.

Katie: When you get your lock, practice the combo until you can open it underwater and blindfolded. Also, enter your number and combo into your phone so you'll always have it. While you're at it, put a red X on your map where your locker is. I promise to think of you tomorrow. Now get some sleep!

Amanda: Thanks so much. Love you!

## [TEXT]

**Amanda:** Good news! I survived day one. I got lost a zillion times but just kept bumping into other lost bodies. It was almost funny. 😂

## [FACETIME]

**Katie:** I told you! Congrats for surviving day one! Only about two hundred ninety left to go, right? And then you'll be laughing at the new kids.

**Amanda:** I didn't think I could change classes without a tour guide today, but it helped to realize that all of us are new.

**Katie:** Of course it does. And think of the freedom. You're not a preschooler holding on to a rope, or an elementary kid silently walking two by two behind a teacher, which always made me think of Noah's Ark! You can walk to class with a friend and visit along the way. Free at last! That's how I met Maria. Remember her?

**Amanda:** Yeah, you brought her to that family trip like last year, right?

**Katie:** Yep! The first day in homeroom we realized we had the same first-period class. We got lost, but at least we got lost together. Now five years later we're best friends. My Spanish teacher can't believe how good my accent is. I don't tell her my secret weapon—a BF who was born in Puerto Rico. So. Big advantage of a huge school. You get to meet lots of new people who don't live in your old neighborhood. Which doesn't mean you lose your old friends.

Amanda: You make it all sound so great. Love you!

### [TEXT]

Amanda: Hey Katie. This morning in math I got slammed! The problems didn't resemble anything I've ever seen before. I think that woman is using some foreign language to explain stuff. I know I'm going to fail. 😬 Can we FaceTime later?

### [FACETIME]

Katie: Oh, Amanda, please calm down. You can do this! How about raising your hand and telling your math teacher that you didn't understand what she was saying?

Amanda: No! I don't want her to think I'm stupid.

**Katie:** You aren't stupid, but you've got to ask for help. It's her job to make you understand what's going on.

**Amanda:** You don't understand how it is, Katie. You're so smart. I didn't get those genes. I take after my mother's side of the family. Long line of English majors. No math genes.

**Katie:** Yes, I'm smart. Smart enough to ask for help when I need it. And I know you are too. Besides, just think how many kids in the class will appreciate your asking a question. They're sitting there too afraid to ask because they don't want people to think they're dumb. You ask the question for them and they'll love you for it, even if they don't say so. Think of it as another way to make friends.

**Amanda:** I wish you'd warned me about how much more work they give you in middle school than elementary. I'm literally drowning in homework.

**Katie:** Three words of advice: *organize, organize, organize.*

**Amanda:** Ouch. Now you're sounding like Mom. I *hate* to organize.

**Katie:** Believe me. Once you make yourself do it, you'll be forever grateful. *Write down* assignments and put on your calendar when they're due. And remember to look at your calendar.

**Amanda:** Yeah. I get it. That's why you're always on the honor roll. I'll try. Thanks.

**Katie:** Love you!

## [TEXT]

**Katie:** Call me. Sob story to share.

## [FACETIME]

**Amanda:** Hi, Katie. What's up?

**Katie:** Here it goes. Long story short, or maybe short story long, last fall we were told at the beginning of art class that a big part of our final grade would be to critique an art show or the work of a single artist in a museum or gallery. I didn't write the assignment down, and when I did think about it, I knew I had plenty of time to get it done. In January my friend Susie asked where I'd gone to do my critique. She'd been to the city art museum and had a ball criticizing some modern guy who just made black splotches on white canvas. I told her I hadn't done it yet. I wanted to learn more about the whole field of art before I wrote it. How's that for a lame excuse? "But it's due tomorrow," she said. What? Tomorrow? How was I going to get to a museum or gallery before they closed that afternoon? Eek! I had soccer practice until five. I caught the late bus home and tried not to cry the whole way. I had an A in art at midterm and I was going to end up failing because of some stupid paper I'd forgotten about. I was full-out bawling when Dad got home from his office. Lucky me.

At work at the hospital, he had noticed that there was an art exhibit in the entrance hall. As you know, hospitals never close. He gave up his basketball game on TV to take me there after supper.

**Amanda:** Oh no! How much did your grade drop in that class?

**Katie:** Luckily it didn't. I had to stay up all night writing the paper, so I was a mess at the game the next day. My poor coach had to take me out for a sub, but I did get the paper in on time. I'll never do that again! Even though my art teacher thought it was "so creative" of me to "think outside the box" and go to see the work of an artist outside the usual venues like galleries and museums. I might well have discovered an up-and-coming genius whose work would be on museum walls one day. Besides, art should belong where ordinary people will see it and begin to appreciate its value. Blah. Blah. Blah. Well, you can bet I didn't tell her *why* I'd chosen the hospital exhibit or *when* or *whose* idea it was. But I'm not counting on that kind of luck to happen again. I nearly died of stress before those twenty-four hours were over. Don't do what I did, Amanda. Be more organized, I beg you!

**Amanda:** Wow! Thanks. I have a calendar on my phone. I guess I better use it.

**Katie:** Now you're talking! Bye for now. Love you!

## [TEXT]

**Amanda:** Just got an essay back from my English teacher. Ogre makes us write one every week. Full of red marks. And I spell-checked it and everything

**Katie:** Spell-check conversation! 👧

## [FACETIME]

**Katie:** Hi, Amanda.

**Amanda:** Hey thanks for calling. I'm so lost.

**Katie:** Don't worry about it. I did the same thing,

and I learned the hard way. Do not rely on spell-check! It does not always work. If it's a word in the dictionary it will pass over it, even if it is not the word you meant. Like *their* for *there* or vice versa. I think the ogre would call it cheating if your English major mother wrote your essay, but he probably wouldn't mind if she checked your spelling before you handed your paper in.

**Amanda:** I just wish everything weren't so hard. I'm already tired, and I've only been at Elm Street Middle School three weeks. I'm really having trouble keeping up.

**Katie:** I'm so sorry to hear it. But you're smart, and you'll do just fine in middle school. Yes, the work is harder and there's more homework. But try to think of it as a challenge—just like soccer. It's more fun if your opponent is really good, right? It's the close games—the ones you win by the skin of your teeth—that are exciting and that you remember with pride.

**Amanda:** I guess that's true. Thanks, Katie. I'll try. I really will. I don't know what I'd do without you. Love you!

## [FACETIME (after 3 missed calls)]

**Katie:** Hi, cuz. Is something wrong?

**Amanda:** I don't think I'm trying out for soccer. Everyone says that the sixth-grade team stinks— and I won't have a chance to play junior varsity. I think I'll just stick with league soccer for now.

**Katie:** What you're hearing about the sixth-grade team may not be true. 👧

**Amanda:** Trying out for the soccer team just doesn't feel good to me. What do you think I should do? Should I try something else?

**Katie:** Here's the great thing about middle school: There are so many other things you might want to try besides soccer. In a school that size, they must have lots of clubs—drama, chorus, orchestra. If you're still playing a horn, the music teacher will love you! Lucas hated middle school until someone—could it have been his awesome sister?—steered him toward the school newspaper. When my brother saw his first story in print, he was suddenly the most devoted booster of middle school—the place he'd sworn he'd hate forever.

**Amanda:** Do you think I should audition for the fall musical? Would a first-year have a chance?

**Katie:** Listen. You're a good singer and a pretty fair dancer. If you want to audition, go for it! You won't be cast if you don't try out. And who knows, you might just get a part. Think about it, and good luck! Love you!

## [TEXT]

**Amanda:** ! You'll never believe it! I'm in the school play! Just the chorus but it is SO much fun! 😃

**Katie:** Congrats! When's the performance? I'll come if I can. I know Mom and Dad would love to come too. Even Lucas might tag along.

**Amanda:** It's December 15 and 16 but it's just a middle school musical. And I'm only in the chorus. No big deal.

**Katie:** I beg to differ. You're a big deal to us!

• • •

**Amanda:** THANK YOU for coming to the show. We weren't supposed to look out at the audience but I couldn't help seeing all of you. Our family took up most of the second row! You guys are so awesome. xxxoooo Merry Christmas! 🙈💙 Let's talk over the holidays.

Katie: Yes!! Merry Christmas! 🎄

## [FACETIME]

Amanda: Hi, Katie. I can't believe I have so much homework to do over the holidays! I haven't finished reading my book for English. And I should do some review in math. I did okay on my midterm report, but finals are coming up a few weeks after New Year. I spent a lot of time in rehearsals for the show, so I let a few things slide.

Katie: Okay, I get it with the work, but you've got to have some fun, too. That's what holidays are for!

Amanda: Don't worry! A bunch of us are planning a New Year's Eve party. My parents offered our house. Sounds generous, right? But we all know it's so they can keep an eye on things. They don't know a lot of the kids who'll be coming—you were right. I have made new friends at school. But even with the hawk eyes in residence, it's the first time I'll have an actual New Year's party.

Katie: That sounds awesome, Amanda! And it's so good to hear about your new friends. I knew you could do it. You're the best! Love you!! Happy holidays!

**[TEXT]**

Amanda: I got my semester grades today. Not all As like you, but good enough. I survived my first semester and I actually like it. You really helped me. Thanks!

Katie: You're the one who did it, Amanda. You go girl! 👏 🖤

**Katherine Paterson** is the internationally acclaimed author of many beloved books for kids, including *Bridge to Terabithia* and *Jacob Have I Loved,* both of which won the Newbery Medal. Born in Qingjiang, China, she has two older and two younger siblings, and together the family moved all over the country and all over the world. Reading and writing have always been her favorite activities, and in sixth grade, in Winston-Salem, North Carolina, she started writing plays for her friends and herself to act out during recess. She makes her home in Montpelier, Vermont, where she is an activist for education and literacy. She has four children, seven grandchildren, and a faithful dog named Pixie.

**Jordan Paterson** attends high school in New Canaan, Connecticut. She is the goalie for her high school varsity soccer team, and she loves to sing and play guitar. She has a brother in college and a dog named Scout. Katherine Paterson is her grandmother. "TBH I Need HELP!! 🙈 " is their first professional collaboration.

# Dog People

## BY LINDA SUE PARK
## AND ANNA DOBBIN

The squirrels were terrorizing the front yard.

I watched them from the chair by the window. As they ran up and down the big tree, they knocked loose some of the old leaves, which drifted to the ground. I figured I might have to help Lucy make the leaves into a pile later. It wasn't my favorite thing to do, but I'd take any chance to spend time with Lucy.

We're best friends, you see.

Just then, I saw her coming up the street more quickly than usual, jogging like she does when she chases me at the park.

I heard Alpha Mom stand up from her desk at the back of the house. I glanced out the window one more time to see that Lucy was still running. She was almost home!

*Squirrels, you have not seen the last of me.*

I jumped down from the chair, then went to sit by the door—near, but not *too* near, like I'm supposed to anytime someone comes to the house.

Alpha Mom appeared in the doorway to the kitchen and looked at me.

"Good boy, Kimchi," she said. "Good boy!"

Lucy rushed into the house and dropped her backpack just inside the door.

"MOM!" she yelled.

"I'm right here, and my hearing is excellent," Mom said from the kitchen doorway.

"Oh—I didn't see you. Wait till I tell you. It's so cool!"

Meanwhile, Kimchi was wagging his tail and grinning and making happy whining noises, so Lucy bent down and scratched his neck and ears. "You listen to this, too, Kimchi—you're gonna love it! Mom, guess what, guess what?"

Mom held up her hands. "I have an email that I absolutely have to finish. How about you pick up the backpack and make us both a snack. By that time I'll be done, and I promise you my undivided attention."

"Okay," Lucy said. She grabbed the pack and heaved it into her arms. It weighed a ton. Not for the first time, she wondered if textbook publishers got paid by the pound.

Pack neatly stowed, Lucy went into the kitchen and did what she thought of as "spelunking" in the fridge. The house rule was healthy snacks between meals, treats for dessert. Lucy got out cheese and crackers and grapes, all of which she liked. Still, she rolled her eyes and muttered, "There's never anything *good*."

Mom came back into the kitchen just in time to hear. "If by 'good' you mean 'of minimal nutritional value,' there's ice cream"—pause, Mom-glare—"for *after* supper."

"Fine." Lucy popped a grape into her mouth. "Just listen. At school today, last period was Club Assembly. For the sixth graders. We went to the cafeteria, and there were all these booths for the school clubs. And we got to go around and talk to the seventh and eighth graders who are members and sign up for the clubs we're interested in." She waved a piece of cheese in the air. "There are so many! Geology Club, Chess, Cooking, Gardening—it was crazy!"

Mom got that look on her face, the one where she was frowning but not letting it show. "Luce, you're already pretty busy," she said. "You've got trumpet and tai chi. That might be enough. Plus, you're going to have more homework than you did last year."

"I knew you'd say that," Lucy said between bites of cheese. "I like being busy, but I don't want to be stressed, so I only joined one."

Pause.

"Okay, tell me," Mom said. "I can't bear the suspense."

Lucy bent over to pick up Kimchi. Kimchi was a pound puppy, a mutt with traces of terrier. He was what Mom called a "one-arm dog," meaning that he could be picked up with one arm. He was perfect— not just in size, but in every way, as far as Lucy was concerned.

Lucy cradled Kimchi like a baby. "Animal Welfare Club! I joined Animal Welfare Club, yes I did! What do you think of that, Kimchi?"

Kimchi wagged his tail and kissed her, then sniffed at her hand. Lucy put him back down on the floor. He promptly sat at her feet and tilted his head. It was his "I'm NOT begging for cheese, nope, not me; I'm *such a GOOD dog* that I'd never even *think* of begging for cheese" look.

Lucy laughed. She kissed the top of his head and gave him a little piece of cheese. "Sudipta joined too. We're all supposed to bring in photos of our pets to the first meeting, and come up with fund-raising ideas. We're raising money for the Way Station Animal Shelter. And we meet on Tuesdays, when I don't have trumpet or tai chi, so it works out just right, see?"

"I believe I'm being informed, not asked," Mom said, "but I'll answer anyway. You can try it for a while and we'll see how it goes." Then she smiled. "It sounds great, Lucy. Right up your alley."

"No—right up my dog run!"



On Tuesday morning, Lucy carefully tucked her favorite photo of Kimchi into the middle of a crisp new notepad. The pad was the size of a pack of index cards, with a paw print on the cover—perfect for taking notes during Animal Welfare Club meetings.

Lucy flipped to the front of the pad. Mmm, that new-paper smell was the best! Well, almost new. She'd written down a bunch of fund-raising ideas on the first page: *Hold a bake sale. Offer pet-sitting and dog-walking services. Rake leaves.*

Even though the seventh and eighth graders had more club experience, Lucy was determined to become a valuable member, starting with today's fund-raiser discussion. The other sixth graders would probably leave the talking to the older kids. But Lucy had thought hard about her ideas, and she intended to share them. Loudly.

Lucy didn't believe in doing anything halfway. She wanted to be a real presence in Animal Welfare Club. Maybe in two years, she'd even be club president. . . .

As she boarded the school bus, Lucy saw Sudipta, her best friend—her best *human* friend, to be precise— waving from a seat near the middle of the bus. They always tried to avoid sitting too close to the crazy eighth-grade boys in the back.

"Which pic of McGonagall did you bring?" Lucy asked, plopping down and bumping shoulders with her friend.

Sudipta pulled a folder from her backpack and opened it. Inside was a photo of a tabby cat lounging across two fluffy pillows on Sudipta's bed.

Lucy laughed. "Look at her! She's in ultimate princess mode."

"I know, right? My dad always says it's McGonagall's house—we're just living in it."

Sometimes a grown-up would declare that they were a dog person or a cat person. Lucy and Sudipta agreed that this was ridiculous. Why choose? They loved dogs, cats, and *all* animals. When they were little kids, they even used to rescue spiders and other bugs they found inside by taking them outside. And Sudipta was a vegetarian. Lucy didn't eat meat often either . . . but she made an exception for her grandma's irresistible bulgogi.

When they got to school, the day flew by faster than a greyhound. It was only their third week back, early enough in the year that everything still felt exciting. Lucy thought she was getting the hang of switching rooms for every class, and she loved exchanging notes on the whiteboard in Sudipta's locker. (They knew each other's combinations, of course.)

After last period, Lucy loaded up her backpack with all the books she needed to do her homework, then headed to Mr. Mendoza's classroom for Animal Welfare Club. Sudipta was already there. Lucy slid into the desk next to her.

Mr. Mendoza, the Spanish teacher, sat at the front of the room, tapping away on his laptop. Lucy had learned at Club Assembly that Animal Welfare Club was student run, but Mr. Mendoza was the faculty advisor.

Sudipta leaned over to whisper into Lucy's ear. "He's been doing that since I got here. He hasn't said hi to anyone."

"Maybe he's like McGonagall," Lucy whispered back. "He ignores you unless you feed him."

They giggled together. Sudipta's giggles always ended in a snort. Lucy would know that snort anywhere.

"Hi, everyone," said a voice by the windows. "If you could take a seat and turn your desks this way, please . . ."

Everyone rotated their desks ninety degrees to face the windows, so now Mr. Mendoza was off to the side. A pale freckled girl with red braids and glasses stood next to a boy with medium-brown skin and a backward baseball cap.

Eighth graders. They seemed so . . . *tall.*

The girl took a breath and began, "I'm Grace, and this is Tarek. We're the copresidents of Animal Welfare Club."

"Thanks for coming, you guys," said Tarek. "Let's start by going around and introducing ourselves."

"And tell us about any pets you have!" Grace added.

"I'll go first. I'm Tarek, and *this*"—he pulled his phone from his jeans pocket and held it up—"is my ball python, Romeo."

Lucy gasped and clutched Sudipta's forearm. On Tarek's phone screen was a close-up of a coiled snake in a glass aquarium. The snake had beady eyes and intricately patterned greenish-brown skin.

"*So* cool," Lucy whispered.

"Romeo is nonvenomous," Tarek went on. "He's two years old, and he could live up to thirty years." Then he pocketed his phone and nodded at Sudipta, who was sitting nearest to him, indicating that she should talk next.

She cleared her throat. "I'm Sudipta. My cat is—"

"Hold on. *What* is your name?"

Lucy's head snapped toward the voice. It belonged to a boy with blond hair and wide-set blue eyes who was sitting a few desks down.

"Um. Su-dip-ta," she repeated.

"That's an *unusual* name," the boy said—sort of unkindly, Lucy thought.

She turned her gaze back to Sudipta and raised an eyebrow as if to say, *What a jerk!* Lucy wanted to show her support; she knew Sudipta was a little sensitive about her name. Some people thought "Sudipta" was hard to remember or pronounce, and they would tease her about it. Once, Sudipta had complained to Lucy, "Ugh! Seriously? It's no harder than, like, *Samantha*."

"For now we're talking one at a time," Grace cut in.

Sudipta glanced at her gratefully, then continued, telling the group about how her family had rescued McGonagall as a kitten, seven years ago. Lucy's turn came next, and she showed everyone the picture from Kimchi's last birthday. She'd put a pointy party hat on Kimchi's head, then captured the exact moment when he was licking frosting off his muzzle.

"Store-bought frosting has lots of artificial ingredients," the blue-eyed boy interrupted. *Again.* "You shouldn't feed it to a dog. . . ." He looked around anxiously, as if there were a dog in peril from frosting at that very moment.

"William."

Everybody looked over at Mr. Mendoza. *He speaks!*

"Please wait your turn, same as in class," he said.

Lucy raised her chin. "Well, for your information, it wasn't store bought. I made the frosting myself from natural peanut butter and coconut oil, which are safe for dogs."

William didn't acknowledge this. He just stared at his desk.

Who was this guy? Did he think Lucy was stupid? He probably didn't even *know* you could make frosting for dogs—clearly she knew a lot more about dogs than he did.

"Okay, um, next?" Tarek said, breaking the awkward silence.

The rest of the club members introduced themselves. There were twelve students in all, and Lucy diligently recorded each person's name and their pet's name in her notepad. Most kids owned a dog or a cat, but one boy had a turtle, and one girl had a goldfish, because— Lucy wrote this down—"My parents won't let me get a piranha."

When William spoke, Lucy locked eyes with Sudipta and purposely tried to ignore what he was saying. She did catch that he had a golden retriever. "I call her Polly, which is short for Polynomial," he said.

Lucy couldn't help rolling her eyes. She leaned over and whispered in Sudipta's ear, "That's an *unusual* name for a dog." Sudipta snorted again.

After the introductions, Grace and Tarek led a brainstorming session for the fund-raiser. When a seventh grader suggested a bake sale and the group agreed, Lucy was both pleased and disappointed—that had been *her* idea, and she wished she'd suggested it first. They set the bake sale date for the Saturday after next, then divided up the tasks: baking, making posters to hang up around school, buying napkins and paper plates.

Lucy volunteered to bake. She loved baking and had some seriously killer recipes up her sleeve—including one for dog treats, which Kimchi went wild for. Not wanting to miss another chance to voice an idea, Lucy raised her hand.

"What if we also sold pet treats?" she said. "I know how to make dog treats, and I bet people would buy them."

"That's a great idea," Grace said.

Murmurs of agreement came from the other club members, and Lucy smiled, sitting up taller. She glanced at William. He didn't even seem to be paying attention; he'd taken out his phone and was tapping on the screen.

Whatever. She knew the club would make a fortune selling her tasty creations. And she'd show William just how amazing—and perfectly *safe*—her homemade dog treats were.

The whole place smelled *really* good. (Not quite as good as bulgogi night—that's my favorite.) When my humans heat up food, the scent reaches every part of the house. Sometimes I can even smell it when I'm outside.

It's enough to drive a dog crazy.

I sat in one place and kept my eyes on Lucy for so long, I almost turned into a statue. (Yes, I know what a statue is. There's one in the park where we go for walks, a woman wearing a blindfold and holding up two food bowls tied together. Statues are useful. They make good places to, you know, raise your leg.)

Anyway. There I was, fixed on watching Lucy, sitting patiently like a good boy, the *goodest* boy. A little quiver, a little drool—otherwise, I might as well have been a statue.

That, my friends, is *focus*.

Lucy was mixing up foods and heating them. I heard her tell Alpha Mom what she was making: cookies for humans and treats for dogs. When Lucy makes food, she hardly ever drops or spills anything. That's why I was concentrating so hard: I had to be alert for the rare times that something hit the floor.

It's my job to clean it up. I can't let the team down.

Lucy made a batch of dog treats first. Nothing fell, not a single crumb. I couldn't help whining, just once.

"Do they smell good, Kimchi?" she asked.

I barked. *Yes! They smell delicious! But don't you think I should taste one, just to be sure?*

Humans are appallingly inefficient communicators—their language has SO MANY WORDS. Dogs can cram a whole lot of meaning into a single bark.

"These are still hot. I'll give you one when they cool down." She put the tray full of treats on the table.

The table.

*The treats. Were on. The table.*

I wasn't allowed on the table. Alpha Mom had made that very, very clear during my first week here. It was confusing, because the table had chairs around it. The chairs' obvious function was to provide aid in reaching the table, but Alpha Mom seemed oblivious to this. The way humans live is often confusing. Usually you have to just roll with it.

Now, further confusion. The treats were *dog* treats. Lucy had made them before. Considering I am the only dog in the household, it was totally reasonable for me to assume that the treats were mine.

Lucy left the kitchen in search of tape and ribbon—something about wrapping things to make them look nice. I hesitated for a moment.

Climbing on the table: *bad.*

Saving Lucy the trouble of feeding me the treats: *good.*

The moment was a short one.

A quick jump onto one of the chairs. An easy step from there to the tabletop. The tray of treats right in front of me.

*Ouch. Hot. But tasty. If you crunch them up—like this—really fast—keep things moving in your mouth—then they won't burn you—*

*Gobble gobble—crunch crunch gulp—*

"KIMCHI!"

Oops.

Rats.

I jumped down quickly. *The table thing, right? I should have dragged the tray off the table—would that have been better?*

"KIMCHI, NO! All of them? You ate ALL of them?"

She said it like it was a bad thing.

(Later it turned out that she was right, sort of. But I'm getting ahead of myself.)

"Kimchi, how could you?" she wailed.

What followed was a loud and unhappy conversation between the three of us. Lucy and Alpha Mom talked, while I contributed a whine or two.

". . . don't have enough for another batch—"

"—have to make a run for supplies—"

"—never thought he would. He's usually so good—"

And then I got gated. Shut out of the kitchen. Prevented from doing my job. That was bad enough, but worse was that Lucy smelled upset.

I hate it when she's sad, or angry, or scared. I always know right away because she smells different. I can't describe what's different; my ability to distinguish smells is so much better than humans' that their language doesn't have the right words. Maybe it would be like trying to describe music to someone who has never heard music before. Try it and you'll see what I mean about smells.

Anyway. Lucy didn't smell right, and I wanted to go to her, to give her a nuzzle or a snuggle. But nope—I was gated.

Things couldn't get any worse, right? Wrong. A little while later, I threw up the treats. Yeah, maybe I ate a few too many. I'll admit I'm not always the best judge of portion size.

Throwing up is a good thing. It makes your stomach feel better. But no matter how many times it happens, Lucy and Alpha Mom refuse to understand this.

Sheesh.

CALM DOWN, EVERYONE.

IT'S JUST VOMIT.

On Saturday morning, Mom drove Lucy and Kimchi to the middle school, with Kimchi's head out the car window the whole way. Every Saturday, there was a farmers' market in the school parking lot. Mr. Mendoza had gotten permission to situate the bake sale nearby, so hopefully the foot traffic from the market would mean lots of customers.

When Lucy stepped out of the car with Kimchi and waved good-bye to Mom, the bake sale was already almost completely set up.

There was a long table with chairs lined up behind it, balloons tied to each end, and a big poster-board sign in front: *ANIMAL WELFARE CLUB BAKE SALE!*

Lucy hurried toward the group. As she got closer, she saw a golden retriever and a black Pomeranian leashed to the school's flagpole. And the dog owners weren't the only people who had brought their pets. Keisha's goldfish was in its bowl on one end of the table; Jason sat in the grass feeding his turtle a banana; and Romeo, Tarek's python, slithered around in its portable aquarium.

Tarek had explained at the last meeting that bringing pets to the bake sale was a marketing strategy. Kids who came over to look at the animals might buy a baked good or two. Lucy had written *Marketing!* in her notepad and circled it. If she wanted to become club president someday, these were the types of things she had to learn.

Lucy rushed up to Grace. "Sorry I'm late."

"That's okay," Grace said. "Is this Kimchi? He's so cute!" She knelt, and Kimchi sniffed her hand.

"Where should I set up my stuff?"

Grace stood and pointed toward the table. "There's room on the left side. We bought plastic platters at the dollar store, so just grab one and lay out your cookies on it. Take this"—she handed Lucy an index card—"and write down the name of your baked goods and how much they are, and tape it to the table in front of your platter. We can help you with pricing if you're not sure."

Lucy walked to the flagpole and let Kimchi say hello to the other dogs. From the first club meeting, she knew the golden belonged to William, and the Pom was Grace's. After a minute of butt-sniffing, Kimchi lay down next to the golden like they had been BFFs for years, and Lucy was slightly dismayed. But then she shook her head. Just because their dogs liked each other didn't mean she had to like William. She secured Kimchi's leash to the pole, then went to the table, just a few yards away.

"There you are!" Sudipta said. Squares of her mom's famous coconut cake were already piled high on a platter. No sign of McGonagall, though—she was strictly a house cat, preferring fluffy pillows, regular meals, and central air-conditioning to the outdoors.

Lucy scooted a chair up to the table. "Kimchi was *sooo* bad last night," she said. She told Sudipta about the snarfing-and-barfing episode.

Sudipta snorted.

"It was *not* funny," Lucy said, but she started laughing too.

Just then, William appeared on her other side. The table was full, so there was nowhere else to move. *Great,* Lucy thought. *Why do I have to be next to* him?

"Hi," he mumbled, then ducked his head, almost as if he didn't want her to say hi back.

"Hello," Lucy answered cautiously.

William sat on a chair and wrote *Lemon Bars* on an index card. Lucy took a plastic platter and arranged her cookies on it. Then she stacked the dog treats, which she had stayed up late rebaking, on another platter.

When she happened to glance toward William again, she noticed him writing a price on his index card: *$1.13.*

"One dollar and thirteen cents?" Lucy blurted.

"Yes," he said, his eyes on the card as he retraced the dollar sign.

She waited for him to continue, but when he didn't, she asked, "Why? You should price them at a whole number, like one dollar."

William taped the index card in front of his lemon bars. "But I did all the calculations," he said. "Cost of the ingredients, an hour and a half of labor, and how much profit I want to make."

"Labor!" Lucy exclaimed. "How did you—"

"Minimum wage," he said. He peeled the index card off the table, straightened it, and pressed it down again.

Lucy was torn between being interested in his answer and annoyed that he had interrupted her. She tried one more time. "If the price is a round number, it'll be easier for people to pay," she said.

"That doesn't make sense," he said. "I already worked it out, and numbers don't lie."

Lucy frowned. "I think we should do what's best for the club," she said. "That's the main thing, right?" She was done being patient with weird William.

He shrugged. "It's already on the card."

Exasperated, Lucy rolled her eyes and muttered, "So make another one. That's stupid."

Sudipta's eyes widened in surprise, and Lucy instantly regretted her rude words. She felt her cheeks flush, but she couldn't bring herself to apologize. After all, William had been impolite to her in the past and not said sorry.

Luckily, it seemed as though he might not have heard her. He was looking over his shoulder, toward the flagpole.

"Ooh, lemon bars! I'll take two."

A woman had approached the table. William placed two bars on a napkin and handed them to her. "One dollar and thirteen cents?" the woman said with a chuckle. She gave him three dollars. "Just keep the change." Then she walked away without even looking at Lucy's offerings.

Lucy bristled and sank an inch lower in her chair. It was going to be a long morning.

I liked Polly the second I smelled her.

Same as with humans, with certain dogs you just *know*.

*My human*, I communicated to Polly by staring at Lucy.

*Mine*, she replied by looking at the boy next to Lucy.

That's how it goes when dogs talk. A lot of body language.

*Did you drive here in a car?* I asked.

*We walked,* she said. *Our dwelling is close.*

*I love getting out of the house.*

*Me too. The sunshine feels most excellent.*

Like a lot of big dogs, Polly was super chill. I hate to say it, but smaller dogs are often kind of twitchy. Don't get me wrong—I'm a small dog myself and have plenty of friends my size. Maybe we have to be more careful about meeting new folks precisely *because* we're smaller, and, well, some of us get a little hyper about it.

The Pom, for example. I knew she belonged to the girl that Lucy had talked to when we first got here—I'd smelled her scent on the girl's hand.

*What's your story, then?* I asked her.

She flipped onto her back and wriggled in the grass. *Grass is the best!* she declared. Then she had a sneezing fit. Then: *Isn't grass the best? Grass, grass, grass!*

Not as hyper as some small dogs I've met. But definitely a few treats short of a full box, if you get my meaning.

After a couple minutes, I caught a whiff of the wrong kind of Lucy smell. She was sitting at the table, staring at Polly's boy. I whined a little.

*What's going on?* Polly asked.

*Lucy smells upset.*

I didn't want to tell her that the cause seemed to be *her* human. Then Polly got to her feet. Her ears were up; she was clearly focused on her boy.

*William is all right when he can depend on routine,* she said. *At home or at school. But when things are new or unfamiliar, sometimes he needs me. This is school, I know, but it's not a school day.*

She watched her boy closely for another minute. When he looked back at her, his expression was serious but loving, and my instinct told me he was a good person. I wondered what he'd done to make Lucy so annoyed with him.

Then a woman walked up to the table, and the boy turned around again.

Polly lay down. *Looks like he's okay now.*

*What happens when he's not?* I asked.

*You know. The usual. Except, like, more. He used to get upset and stay that way for ages. Now, when he starts to smell upset, I go to him and put my paws on his shoulders, and I push him down gently, so we end up on the floor together and have a cuddle. Afterward, he usually smells okay again.*

*What makes him upset?*

*Sometimes other people. Sometimes just himself—he gets frustrated. But he loves animals, so I'm lucky there. He thinks I'm the greatest.*

I knew exactly what she meant.

Meanwhile, the Pom had been flouncing in circles, winding her leash around the pole we were tied to. She'd run out of leash, but she kept tugging in the same direction, instead of reversing, which would have untangled her.

Finally she quit struggling and slumped over, tuckered out, with her face smooshed against the pole.

She gave a whimper: *Aw, jeez, not again. Little help, please?*


On Tuesday afternoon, rain lashed against the windows of Mr. Mendoza's classroom. Lucy opened her Animal Welfare Club notepad and wrote the date neatly in the top-right corner of a fresh page.

"First things first," Grace said. "Thank you guys so much for an amazing bake sale. We crushed it!"

"Our grand total is . . . ," Tarek began. "Can I get a drumroll, please?"

Everyone thumped their palms against the desks. The sound matched the pitter-patter of the raindrops.

"One hundred and eighty-three dollars!" Tarek shouted.

The group cheered. Lucy high-fived Sudipta, then recorded the number in her notepad.

"We also want to congratulate William for being the highest earner," Grace said. "His lemon bars sold out."

Not only had they sold out, but Lucy had watched as customer after customer gave William *more* than $1.13 for each bar. "Keep the change," over and over.

Lucy huffed. She wasn't sure whether she was more irked that he'd earned so much money or that she'd been sort of wrong about his weird pricing strategy.

She looked at him. In fact, the whole group had turned to look at him—but he wasn't paying attention. He was slouched in his seat, staring at his phone and tapping the screen with both thumbs, like he was playing a game.

Grace cleared her throat. "Great job, William," she said loudly.

"Thanks," he mumbled, without taking his eyes off his phone.

Tarek and Grace turned toward each other and shrugged.

"We're going to Way Station this Saturday to deliver the donation," said Tarek. "If you want to come, take a permission slip for your parents to sign."

The stack of slips went around the room, each person taking one. Out of the corner of her eye, Lucy saw William straighten up when he read the paper.

"We're going to the shelter?" he asked, putting down his phone.

"That's what I just said," Tarek answered.

William sat forward. "To help with the animals?"

"No. We're just going to drop off the donation."

"But we should volunteer while we're there."

"We've gone down that route before," Grace said. "Last year, we asked if we could volunteer as a group. But we're not old enough—you have to be over eighteen. Some of the animals are dangerous, and the shelter doesn't want any kids getting hurt."

William scowled. "It shouldn't matter how old I am. I—I just want to help the animals." He picked up his phone again and clutched it tightly.

"We *are* helping," said Grace. "The shelter always needs money."

Mr. Mendoza spoke then. "William, would you like me to explain it to you in greater detail?"

"In the hallway again," William said with a sigh. He got up and followed Mr. Mendoza out the door.

Lucy, whose eyes had been ping-ponging between the club copresidents and William, shifted her gaze back to her notepad. Surreptitiously, she drew a quick picture of a grumpy cat with a puckered mouth and a collar that said *William*. She wrote *What a sourpuss!* underneath, then slid the notepad toward Sudipta, who stifled a giggle.

"Don't be mean," Sudipta whispered.

Lucy shrugged, but she scribbled out the drawing.

Mr. Mendoza and William came back in. The club members spent the rest of the meeting making a big card to accompany the donation. William sat quietly, staring at his phone.

As Lucy set to work cutting out pictures of animals printed from the Internet, she thought about how the staff at the shelter would react to receiving their donation. They would probably want to get a group photo with the club. Maybe they would do a story for their website. Or put the club members' names on the Wall of Donors.

Hopefully William wouldn't find a way to ruin the experience.

Deep in my bones, I could feel thunder coming.

The rain was clattering against the house. When Lucy got home, she was soaked from head to toe.

I greeted her at the door. Alpha Mom, who was in her office, yelled something about changing out of her wet clothes before she caught a cold.

Sometimes Alpha Mom knows things even when she's not in the room. Like that time I got into the kitchen garbage. (Humans throw out perfectly good food all the time. It's tragic.) I swore I was being quiet, but a couple of digs into the bin and she screamed, "I DON'T THINK SO, BUDDY!" from the other side of the house.

It's like she has more sets of eyes than a wolf pack.

I followed Lucy upstairs and jumped onto her bed, waiting for my cuddles. After she changed, she sat next to me and scratched behind my ears. I stepped into her lap.

She smelled normal, just like my Lucy, but I could tell that her emotions were mixed: half excited, half anxious and irritated. When she was younger, her moods were straightforward: happy, sad, angry, scared. Over the last year or so, I'd noticed that her feelings were sometimes more complex. I understood that it was part of her getting older.

But my approach to lifting her spirits had not changed. I started kissing her face.

I felt her body relax, releasing some of that anxiety and irritation.

It was working! More kisses!

And then she laughed—my favorite sound in the world.


Lucy and Sudipta found seats together in the minibus. Ten of the twelve club members were making the trip, but the noise level sounded more like fifty kids.

Even sitting side by side, Lucy had to raise her voice so Sudipta could hear her.

"A hundred eighty-three dollars is a lot!" she hollered.

"I know!" Sudipta shouted back. "I hope they use some of it to spay cats."

Across the aisle, William sat hunched forward with his fingers in his ears and his eyes shut tight. He looked a little peculiar, but Lucy didn't blame him—it was *really* noisy. A few moments later, Mr. Mendoza got on the bus and asked for *silencio*. Everyone quieted down. William sat up straighter and took his fingers out of his ears in obvious relief.

Lucy knew that Tarek and Grace would be the ones to present the card and the check to the shelter. That was fair; they were the club presidents. But maybe she could stand right next to them. She had rehearsed something to say to the shelter people if the chance came up.

*We're proud to support the work you do here.*

She thought it sounded good. Grown-up, but not pompous.

The shelter was a twenty-minute drive from the school. When the van pulled into the parking lot, everyone piled out, talking excitedly.

"Quiet, guys," William said in a loud voice.

*Excuse me?* Lucy thought. *He's top earner, so he thinks he can boss us around?*

"Too much noise might upset the animals," William went on.

*Oh. Well, that's true.*

Mr. Mendoza held the door open while the club members filed in. They were quieter now, but the group still simmered with excitement in whispers, murmurs, smiles of anticipation.

A woman with fair skin, blond-streaked hair, and lavender-framed glasses sat at the reception desk. She was talking on the phone.

". . . already fully booked that week. No. No. I'll let you know if we have a cancellation. That's the best I can do."

She began tapping on her keyboard, then ended the conversation and hung up.

"Can I help you?" she said, still typing.

The phone rang again.

"Way Station Animal Shelter. How can I help you?"

Lucy saw Grace and Tarek looking at each other uncertainly. She glanced at Mr. Mendoza, who stood at the back of the group, his hands in his pockets. He was clearly not going to take the lead here.

Everyone waited until the receptionist had hung up the phone again. Then Tarek and Grace stepped forward.

"Um, we called earlier?" Grace said. "We're from Douglass Middle School, the Animal Welfare Club."

"I'm sorry—you're from where?" The receptionist looked at her computer screen. "You must have spoken to someone else. There's nothing on the schedule. What did you want?"

Her voice was impatient. Lucy was beginning to feel anxious. This was not how things were supposed to be going.

"We brought a donation," Tarek said. He held up the card, and the smaller envelope containing the check.

"Oh, a donation. Just put it in the box."

She pointed at the wall to her right, where there was a large box made of clear plastic with a slot in the top. The box was half full of money. Lucy wondered how much was in there.

"We just—" Tarek started to say, but then the phone rang again. The receptionist answered it, turning her body away from him and the rest of the club members.

Tarek shrugged helplessly. He walked to the box and looked at the slot. It was too small for the big card; he had to fold it twice. Their nice card, all creased now. And when the envelope landed inside, it sort of blended in with the other bills.

Lucy stared at the receptionist, who was putting the

latest caller on hold. She felt like she was about to explode.

*We worked so hard,* she wanted to yell, *and it doesn't seem like you're the least bit grateful! That's the last time we raise money for this place!*

Fists clenched, she held her breath to keep the words from bursting out.

No group photo.

No appreciation.

No chance to say the nice line she had prepared.

Sudipta looked like she was about to cry. Tarek was shaking his head; Grace's eyes were narrowed. Lucy could hear unhappy muttering from the other club members. Mr. Mendoza had walked into the middle of the group, a concerned expression on his face.

The only one who didn't seem the least bit bothered was William.

He was staring at a family with a kid who was maybe a third grader. The family had just walked out of a door at the back of the room—and the kid, a girl in a green dress, was pulling a skittish little dog on a leash. The dog looked like a Yorkie that needed a haircut. It seemed reluctant to follow the family, skidding around on the tile floor and whimpering. A newly adopted dog, Lucy guessed.

The parents stopped at the front desk to ask the

receptionist something. Behind them, the girl bent down to try to pick up the Yorkie. It yipped and circled her legs, wrapping the leash around the girl's knees.

She spun around and tried again, dipping low and reaching for the dog. It pulled away from her, yanking the leash taut, and its body began to quiver.

*Poor thing*, Lucy thought.

"Stop," William said. He didn't say it loud, or mean—just kind of firmly. The girl in the green dress looked up.

Lucy watched William walk over to her. "I could try," he said.

The girl furrowed her brow, a little suspicious, but she nodded.

William moved so he was facing the same direction as the shivering Yorkie, but he didn't look at the dog. Then he squatted about three feet away, still without making eye contact, and waited.

Lucy realized that William was letting the dog come to him—not the other way around. She exchanged a glance with Sudipta, who was standing next to her and watching too.

Several seconds passed; then the Yorkie let up on the leash slightly, allowing it to slacken. It took one, two, three cautious steps toward William.

Slowly, William extended his fist. The dog stretched out its neck and sniffed.

By now the girl's parents had turned around and were watching, their faces showing surprise and interest.

The Yorkie licked one of William's knuckles, then retreated, distancing itself again. It still looked scared, but it wasn't shaking anymore.

William looked up at the girl. "He doesn't want to be touched," he said. "Just keep him on the lead for now. He'll let you pick him up when he's ready."

Then he stood and started walking away, hands in his pockets like it was no big deal. The other club members hadn't seen what happened—they had migrated toward the door, with Mr. Mendoza trying to console everyone.

Lucy watched William glance over his shoulder at the family and their new dog. She felt a twinge of shame, thinking about how angry she'd been just a minute earlier.

Sure, handing over the donation hadn't been as momentous as she had imagined. But raising money had never been about her, or about any of the club members. It was about helping the animals—and William seemed to be the only person who got that part right.

She took a breath and tried to compliment him, or maybe thank him—she wasn't sure *what* to say. "You . . . I mean, that was—"

"Time to go," Mr. Mendoza called, interrupting her. He held the door open again.

William headed straight over and disappeared outside.

Lucy followed, her words caught in her throat.

If I had to choose the best place ever—besides Lucy's lap—it would be *the park.*

That's what Lucy calls it. "Wanna go to *the park*?" she says, usually while dangling my leash in her hand.

Lucy took me there on a day she didn't have school. It was kind of cold—chilly enough that I figured we might not stay too long. So I had to make the most of it. I said hi to *everyone*—old friends and new friends, both canine and human. I sniffed and marked as much territory as I possibly could.

We reached my favorite part of the park—the big empty field with that statue of the lady with the food bowls. And then GUESS who showed up?

*Polly!* I barked. *Hey, Polly, over here!*

Polly barked back a greeting, but unlike me, she wasn't straining against her leash. She guided her boy over gently.

Like I said—*super* chill.

*Salutations, friend,* she said, sniffing my behind. *Lovely day for walkies, isn't it?*

Wagging in agreement, I looked up at Lucy. She

had her eyes on Polly's human—William, that was his name—who was staring at his forearm.

"I have a new FitGizmo," he said.

He hadn't said hello to Lucy, or waved his hand, or done any of the things that seemed to be the human equivalent of butt-sniffing.

"It counts the number of steps I take. When I bring Polly to the park, my daily step count goes up by at least seventy percent."

Lucy was quiet for a moment. I quieted down, too, and went to sit at her feet—I could tell she was slightly uneasy.

"That's cool," she said at last. "William, I didn't get a chance to tell you before. . . . At the shelter? When you helped that girl with her dog? That was—really great."

I saw William's eyes flick up to her face. "I like dogs," he said with a shrug. Then he went back to looking at his arm.

Another short silence. Lucy's forehead was a little wrinkled, but she smelled okay.

"Seventy percent," she said. "Did you figure that out in your head?"

William looked up again. This time, his eyes focused on Lucy.

"Yeah," he said. "My current average is five thousand thirteen steps a day. On park days it goes up to at least eight thousand five hundred. That's about a seventy percent increase."

Hearing the word *park* reminded me—we were in *the park!* This was no time to be sitting still! I gave a short bark and began prancing.

"Want to let them run around together?" Lucy asked.

William didn't reply, but he bent down and unclipped the leash from Polly's harness while Lucy did the same for me.

Joy! Freedom! Run, run, *RUN!*

I chased Polly. Polly chased me. We ran and leapt and tumbled. It was glorious. I felt like I could run forever.

At last our humans whistled to us. Panting, we returned to their sides and had our leashes clipped on again.

Lucy was smiling. "I bet Polly's step count is a lot bigger on park days too."

William tilted his head. "Do you think anyone has ever counted a dog's steps?"

Lucy giggled. "I doubt it. Maybe we could try."

"Okay. I'll figure out a way to count them. I always bring Polly to the park on Sunday afternoons. It'll be interesting to see the differences between their step counts, Polly's and Kimchi's."

I heard that. My name. I cocked my head.

Lucy's eyes met mine. She glanced at Polly, then back at me, and finally up at William. "So . . . we'll meet here next week?" she said.

William and Polly were already walking away. "We come at two o'clock."

Lucy knelt down and scratched behind my ears.

*Ooh. Nice. Just a little to the left—no, the other way—aaah. Bliss.*

"I guess that means yes . . . ," she murmured. She kissed the top of my head. "What do you think? You want to play with Polly again?"

I licked her cheek.

Which also meant yes. Now, and always.

 **Linda Sue Park** is the author of many books for kids, including the Newbery Award winner *A Single Shard* and the *New York Times* bestseller *A Long Walk to Water*. When she was in middle school, she lived with her family in a Chicago suburb; they owned a very smart miniature poodle named Jeffy. She and her co-author, Anna Dobbin, who also happens to be her daughter, are both dog people. They regret their inability to be cat people due to severe allergies.

 **Anna Dobbin** is a writer, copy editor, and proofreader. She owns an adorable Italian greyhound named Pintxo. In middle school she played soccer three hundred days a year and also loved singing, reading, and making art.

Anna is Linda Sue Park's daughter. "Dog People" is their first professional collaboration.

# Middle School
## BY DAVID WIESNER

When I started sixth grade, there were too many kids to fit in the middle schools.

HIGH SCHO

So the school district put all of us into the brand-new, half-full high school.

A couple hundred eleven-year-olds in with kids who were fourteen, fifteen, and sixteen.

The halls were huge. So were the kids.

 **David Wiesner** is best known as the three-time winner of the Caldecott Medal for his awesome wordless picture books: *The Three Pigs, Tuesday,* and *Flotsam.* He also won Caldecott Honors for *Free Fall, Sector 7,* and *Mr. Wuffles!* He grew up in New Jersey as the youngest of five kids and has three sisters and a brother (if you look closely at his picture book *Hurricane,* you will see that the book is dedicated to his siblings and all the art is based on his childhood home and cat, Fuzzy, named Hannibel in the book!). Not surprisingly, drawing was always his passion, along with playing outside, endlessly. He remembers sixth grade as the worst year of his school life, despite being temporarily housed in the high school, with its fully stocked high school art room, memorialized in "Middle School." Happily, seventh and eighth grades got much better for him. He pursued his passion for visual storytelling at the Rhode Island School of Design. David lives and works outside Philadelphia. He and his wife have two grown children.

# ACKNOWLEDGMENTS

How lucky I am! I'm deeply grateful to Beverly Horowitz, dear friend and brilliant VP and editor in chief of Delacorte Press, for offering me this awesome project. My formidable agent and longtime friend Doe Coover brought it home painlessly (for me, anyway) and in record time. Thanks also to editor Kelsey Horton, who jumped on the *TMS* train and never let go!

Emily Meyer at the Cambridge Public Library and Sam Musher and Anna Marsh at the Cambridge Public Schools—on the front lines of middle school every single day—were so helpful to me. Chris Krones provided technical assistance without which this collection wouldn't have happened. Really.

As for gratitude for the generous and talented contributors, each of whom agreed to be part of this worthwhile collection *without a moment's hesitation*? I am, ironically, without words, but with clear eyes and a full heart.

I'm thankful every day for the love and support of friends and family (you know who you are) but will mention by name my remarkable daughters, Phoebe and Hilary. I suppose you already know that everything I do is for you.

# ABOUT THE EDITOR

**Betsy Groban** grew up in a leafy (sometimes lethal) sub-urb outside New York City and is a proud graduate of Bar-nard College, with a degree in English literature. She has always worked at the intersection of culture, commerce, and community—specifically in book publishing, public broad-casting, and arts advocacy. She lives in Cambridge, Massa-chusetts, and has two awesome grown daughters, Phoebe and Hilary.

# TOP 10 THINGS TO DO
# BEFORE MIDDLE SCHOOL

1. Surround yourself with the things that make you feel most like yourself: your favorite outfit, pair of shoes, music, hobby.

2. Choose a new and very cool nickname for yourself.

3. Make sure you know where your bus stop is.

4. Learn your way around school, since you'll be changing classrooms all the time.

5. Memorize the combination of your lock.

6. Find out as much as you can about what happens in gym. And at lunch.

7. Bring a favorite book the first day, just in case.

8. Stick a preschool or kindergarten picture of yourself inside your binder to remind you how far you've already come.

9. Memorize this quote from author/screenwriter/ actor/dancer Tim Federle: "Everything that got me picked on as a middle schooler gets me paid now."

10. B-R-E-A-T-H-E.